Men at Work

First Edition

Published by The Nazca Plains Corporation
Las Vegas, Nevada
2009

ISBN: 978-1-935509-17-2

Published by

The Nazca Plains Corporation ®
4640 Paradise Rd, Suite 141
Las Vegas NV 89109-8000

PUBLISHER'S NOTE
Men at Work is a work of fiction created wholly by *Christopher Trevor's* imagination. All characters are fictional and any resemblance to any persons living or deceased is purely by accident. No portion of this book reflects any real person or events.

Cover Photo, Les Byerley
Art Director, Blake Stephens

Dedication

For David Anthony, who truly reads me and sees between my lines.

Men at Work

First Edition

Christopher Trevor

Table of Contents

Introduction

Greetings Constant Readers and welcome to all new readers of my work. With this, my twenty-seventh published work I would like to pay homage and give respect to all of us that have to work for a living. Namely, or more precisely, I want to offer homage and pay respect to "Men at Work." Bartenders, personal trainers, captains of football teams, plumbers, military reservists and even the guy who shines shoes for a living are all featured in this newest collection of erotic tales that I am pleased to bring to you. Read what happens when "Chuck", a hunky bartender loses his short shorts (yes you read that correctly) while on a bathroom break at the sleazy bar he works in and must pay a hefty price to score them back in the lead story "Chuck the Bartender." Bodybuilders abound in two tales in this book in the stories "Captured Bodybuilder" and "The Bodybuilder." In "Captured Bodybuilder" a muscle bound hunk is shocked to find himself to be the buffet for a group of meat hungry unseen baddies. The story winds out with one of my usual unusual and twisted endings. In "The Bodybuilder" the tables are turned on a dominant top-man when his two wussie sex slaves and two gym members decide to make him the main course for their insatiable hungers. Like with "Captured Bodybuilder" this story also contains an ironic ending…no peeking please…read all the way to the nut-busting ending. No college football team would be complete without their handsome and studly captain and for as long as I can remember nothing is more sinister than capturing the college football team's captain for some erotic horseplay. In stories I have written this is played out wherein members of a losing team manage to kidnap the winning team's captain and make his life miserable in some way for a few hours. In the story "The Captain of the Football Team" horseplay is just what happens…until the horseplay becomes a tad more than what the captain of the football team bargained for…

"The Plumber" could be a real story that happened to the author himself many years ago, but then again, perhaps it is just a figment of the author's imagination or wishful thinking. Either way, this story was inspired by a plumber we all wish would come (cum?) to fix our pipes (pun intended).

In "Shoeshine" a handsome business executive has his erotic kidnap and foot fetish fantasies intertwined when he realizes that he needs his shoes shined before an upcoming business engagement. What should be a routine shoeshine turns into a very intense and heated experience for the handsome executive.

The book winds out with the mini novella "The Meister" starring recurring tickle hero/victim Timmy Backman. In this tale Timmy Backman is on military duty and unwittingly finds himself involved in a case of serial kidnapping and tickling. The story was inspired by the author's poet dreamer buddy and also introduces a new tickle villain, "The Tickle Meister."

As Always, I wish you Happy Reading…

Christopher Trevor

■

Chuck the Bartender

Author's Note:

I don't know what the chances are of what happens in my story "Chuck the bartender" of ever really happening. Who knows, maybe it has happened to some (un) fortunate guys out there. Granted, this story has echoes of my other scantily clad story "The Lifeguard's Red Speedo", which appeared in my book aptly titled "Humiliation." What I do know is that the model for the guy "Chuck the Bartender" in the story was more than a magnificent sight to behold that night at the gay bar that I was hanging out in that summer night in Manhattan. And granted this story sure does make for a great fantasy. I also know what a chance a guy is taking when wearing a pair of very short shorts, a Speedo on the beach, or even those competition briefs (or posing briefs) as they call them that bodybuilding competing weightlifters wear at the public contests they appear in. These scanty items of attire pose many intriguing and sinister possibilities. So much man with so little covering that an erection would be impossible to hide, as in my story, "Ross Smith, Champion (and captive) Body Builder" which appeared in my book "Executive Ties That Bind." It wouldn't take much to remove them. A simple snip with a knife or scissors would make it possible to remove them completely, or if a guy was stunned and off guard for a moment, as in the story you are about to read, easy to yank them off him in one or two quick pulls, leaving the dude thoroughly humiliated and very vulnerable to a host of possibilities. I do not encourage this type of horseplay or joke playing in real life as the consequences can be more than severe, although in the realm of fiction, as a good buddy recently told me, there is no such thing as too sleazy or too erotic.

Happy Reading.

Christopher Trevor

The Story

My name is Howard; I'm twenty-three years old. Recently my two good buddies (Dennis and Rodd) and I had a really fun, sinister and erotic experience that I want to share with you. It was on a Saturday night at a trendy gay bar, which is located in the Chelsea area of Manhattan in New York City. At this particular bar which is made up sort of like a swimming pool area at a posh hotel all the bartenders wear just a G-string or a pair of short shorts or a tight Speedo while tending bar and serving customers drinks. I am sure that you can imagine their bodies. They more than likely have to stay in better than tip-top shape if they want to maintain their jobs at the bar and continue to enjoy the hefty tips the customers bestow upon them. For a twenty, twenty five, or even a fifty dollar tip a muscular bartender might give you the privilege of letting you squeeze one or both of his nipples a few times. If he's hard in his G-string or shorts or Speedo you might earn a quick feel, but that'll be it, just teasing bud, and it would cost you. The bartenders at this bar look like they work out for more than a few hours everyday, what with their pumped up rock hard chests, giant bouncing pecs, wide as a doorway shoulders, muscular arms with biceps the size of bowling balls and tree-trunk like legs, and some of the hardest and muscular butts you'll ever see. I would think based on what I just described to you that these guys workout eight hours a day before taking up position at the appointed posts at the bar. I also wonder how many of these muscle gods take steroids to have their bodies in the shape they are in. Anyway, Dennis, Rodd and I had decided to go to the trendy bar and have a few beers, and then perhaps hit a dance club afterwards. None of us had planned on munching on a particular bartender's man tits and milking his cock that night. And we wouldn't even have to tip big in order to accomplish those things bud. We were standing a few feet away from the front bar, each of us holding a cold bottle of beer in our hands. The bartender was of course hot looking to say the least. He was about five feet nine inches tall, had dark hair cut military style, (real sever buzz cut) dark eyes, and he was muscular from his neck down to his calves with a flat washboard stomach. His belly button was large and deep to the point of being totally erotic looking, His skin looked as soft and smooth as finely spun silk. When he had served us our beers I imagined pushing my tongue deep into that cute belly button of his. No doubt he would react with shudders and chills', seeing as the belly button is a most sensitive area for most guys. I wondered how big a tip I would have to provide to make that fantasy a reality. He was wearing a pair of tight fitting navy blue short shorts, which more than showed off his big meaty bulge and his hot tight buns very nicely. Actually, the sides of his buns were sticking out of the shorts, real provocative looking, they were that tight and perhaps a size small on him. The only other clothing he had on was a pair of sneakers with white sweat socks pushed down around his ankles. As I said, that was all most of the bartenders at that particular bar wore. The bar catered to a very jock type of crowd and was designed as I said like the area of a hotel's swimming pool, but also sort of as a men's locker room, with shower stalls set up over the bars. During late night the bar featured Speedo bikini-wearing muscle boys standing in those stalls taking showers, enough to make you thirsty for plenty to drink. After the bartender had served us our beers we hard another patron say "Thank you Chuck" after he had been served his drink. We stood sipping our beers, looking lustfully at the hot and muscular bartender named Chuck as he served drinks to other patrons of the bar.

"Man oh fucking man he is hotter than hot," Dennis exclaimed. "What I wouldn't give to really work him over for a while."

"I don't think I would be able to stop working him over if I had the chance," Rodd said meanly. "Look at that fucking chest on him. Feast fit for a king, and his goddamned man tits look fucking succulent and delicious."

"And I think he knows it too," Dennis said. "It looks to me like he uses vacuum pumps and snake bight kits to keep them real fat and erect like that."

"Man, I would love to chew on those man tits of his till he couldn't stand it, and then some," Rodd said and took a hearty swig of his beer.

"I would love to get my hands on those shorts of his," I made the mistake of saying. "I'll bet that they smell of his sweaty crotch. Look at how he's running around behind that bar. Fucking guy is sweating like crazy."

"You are a pervert Howard buddy," Dennis said. "All you would want from that hot looking fucker are his damned shorts?"

"You have your fetishes and I have mine," I said defensively but with a smile.

"I have a challenge for you Howard," Dennis said, putting an arm around my shoulder.

"What is it?" I asked him.

"Lean in close here guys, I don't want the whole place hearing this," Dennis said as he, Rodd and I huddled out of earshot. "I dare you to somehow get those shorts he's wearing off him. As a matter of fact I double dare you."

"I fucking triple dare you," Rodd chimed in, sounding as if he could not believe what Dennis had just said. "Shit man, if you can get those shorts off that fucking hunk and a half I'll buy you two beers the next time we come here."

"That's if they let us in again after Howard here steals the bartender's shorts off him," Dennis said with a grin on his face.

"You two *have got to be kidding,*" I said, looking at them like they were totally out of their minds. "What do you think, that he's just going to hand his damned shorts over to me?"

"You can think of a way can't you Howard?" Dennis asked me, taking his hand off my shoulder. "You want them bad enough from the way you were talking about them."

"I-I really don't know," I said, looking longingly at Chuck the bartender's crotch.

"I'm sure he's going to have to take a bathroom break at some point," Rodd said, sounding totally fiendish. "And I know that the employees of this place use a private bathroom which is at the back of the bar."

We all looked at each other and smiled, a wicked idea forming between the three of us. Slowly, we made our way to the back of the bar. A little while later we saw Chuck sauntering real sexily toward the private employee's bathroom. Obviously he was on a break. He walked like someone who was totally confident about himself. His shoulders were raised high and his muscular arms swung like two slabs of beef as he swaggered toward the bathroom.

"Okay Howard, there he is," Dennis said to me.

My heart pounded like crazy in my chest as we watched Chuck go into the private bathroom, which was halfway down a short corridor, away from the crowd and noise of the place. I stood up and walked toward the bathroom. When I got to the door of the bathroom I saw that it was open a crack. I peered in and saw Chuck standing over a toilet in a stall with the door behind him wide open. His shorts were pulled down and bunched around his sexy thighs because they didn't have a fly opening in the front. His butt looked like a bowl of smooth whipped cream. My breath caught in my throat at the sight of that awesome looking butt. I looked more than longingly at those shorts of his bunched around his muscular thighs. It was obvious how moist and sweat soaked they were, as the guy wasn't wearing underpants.

"Go for it," I said to myself. "No one is looking."

I silently pushed the door of the bathroom open and stepped inside. I closed the door, leaving it open just a crack. Chuck was pissing long and heavy into the bowl. His hands were occupied holding his cock so I made my move. I crept up as silently as possible behind the handsome muscle boy bartender and quickly yanked his shorts all the way down to his ankles.

"H-hey!" he roared and his piss splashed on the wall as he lost his balance.

With his piss spurting cock in his hand he turned to face me but his shorts down around his ankles threw him even further off balance. He slid to the floor in front of the toilet.

"Shit!" Chuck hollered as his sexy butt hit the floor and his piss spurted in his pubic bush.

As he was about to try to get up I grabbed his ankles and toppled him again. At the same time I quickly pulled his shorts off him over his sneakers and sweat socks.

"H-hey, *just what the fuck do you think you're doing man?"* Chuck yelled angrily as I relieved him of his shorts.

As he was getting up I ran to the door with his shorts in my hand.

"Come back here with my damned shorts you sleazy bastard!" Chuck yelled threateningly.

I stepped out of the bathroom, closing the door behind me.

"Hey, get back here!" Chuck yelled from behind the door. *"Fucker!"*

He pounded angrily on the door but I knew that he would not come running out all balls ass naked. Holding Chuck's prized and damp shorts in my hand I stole a sniff of them and walked back over to Dennis and Rodd.

"So, did you chicken out?" Dennis asked me snidely.

Smiling fiendishly I held up Chuck's shorts and slyly said, "Got them."

"Holy fucking shit!" Dennis said in total shock. *"Holy fuck, you really did get that fucking hunk's shorts off him.* Where is he now?"

"Still in the bathroom I suppose," I replied. "I mean, where else could he possibly be?"

Dennis and Rodd looked at each other and smiled.

"Come on Rodd, lets go get that guy," Dennis said sounding real lustful.

As we walked over to the door of the private bathroom I stuffed Chuck's shorts into my jeans pocket. Chuck was still yelling and bellowing for me to return his shorts when Dennis and Rodd walked into the bathroom. I stood guarding the door so to speak. At the sight of my two buddies entering the bathroom Chuck quickly put his hands over his big meaty cock and juicy balls.

"Who the fuck are you two?" Chuck asked, standing there feeling totally awkward. "This is a private bathroom for employees only."

"We know, and so does our buddy who confiscated your shorts chucky boy," Dennis said as he and Rodd approached the overly hunky bartender.

"What do you fuckers want?" Chuck asked, still holding his hands over his crotch. "Fuckers, I saw you guys out at the bar checking me out. This was what you planned huh? To have your buddy come in here and steal my damned shorts off me…"

"What do you think we want?" Dennis asked him and hooked a hand onto one of Chuck's bowling ball like biceps.

"Bastards," Chuck rasped as Rodd took his other arm.

Together, Dennis and Rodd pulled Chuck's muscular arms towards themselves, pulling his big hands away from his cock and balls. The bartender's cock was as hard as a rock, fat and long, pointing straight ahead as it twitched around, oozing pre cum from his wide and sexy slit. The sausage like thing was tremendously veiny up and down the sides of his shaft. His big juicy balls were hanging low and sweaty in his hairless sac. Muscular as he was he could have pulled away from my two buddies and kicked both their asses right there on the spot, but, stripped as he was and with nowhere to go I supposed that he was feeling a little more than vulnerable at that moment.

"Damn it Chuck, with a meat stick that size you shouldn't keep it covered up," Rodd said, holding the bartender's muscular arm with two hands, caressing it. "You should be proud of that jumbo-sized cock of yours. And how can we resist that?"

"I'm going to kick both your asses, and then I'm going to get your perverted shorts-stealing buddy," Chuck yelled at them and his cock oozed more pre cum.

"How?" Dennis asked him. "Are you going to go running out into that crowded bar like this?"

Dennis gave one of Chuck's big fleshy nipples a squeeze.

"Shit, I should have locked myself in a damned stall," Chuck ranted angrily, glancing down as Dennis tweaked his fat nipple.

"We could have gotten you out of there instantly," Dennis said.

"Just what the fuck do you guys want?" Chuck asked them again.

"You let us chow on those hot man tits of yours for a while and maybe get you off a few times, and then we'll see about telling our buddy to return your shorts so you can walk out of here," Dennis replied.

"Yeah, and he'll even put the shorts on you with his own two hands," Rodd added mockingly.

As my two buddies spoke Chuck's cock twitched big and meaty between his muscular legs. And then, without another word the muscular bartender placed his hands up behind his head, crossing them. Dennis and Rodd leaned forward and they each slurped one of Chuck's big nipples into their mouths.

"Ohhhhhrrrrrr fuckers," Chuck groaned as they sucked and slurped his nipples real hard.

They caressed and rubbed his stomach region, feeling up his muscular body as they worked and worked his nipples harder and harder.

"Fuckers better return my damned shorts after this," Chuck said breathlessly. "Working me over like I'm a damned piece of meat or something."

Chuck lowered his hands and placed them on the backs of Dennis and Rodd's necks, swooning as he did so. As they sucked heartily on his nipples Chuck caressed and squeezed the backs of their necks.

"Ohhhhhhhh yeah," Chuck moaned in ecstasy. "If you wanted my nips so bad all you had to do was say so. You know that a nice big hefty tip would've earned you some good sucks at my man tits."

Dennis and Rodd each kissed Chuck on the lips a few times, their tongues darting in and out of the muscle boy bartender's mouth and then went back to working on his nipples. Dennis helped himself and tugged on Chuck's big sweaty balls, squeezing them.

"Bet you'd like us to work on those big fat goose egg balls of yours huh Stud?" Dennis asked Chuck.

Chuck simply looked angrily at Dennis. Without another word Dennis and Rodd slid to their knees and each of them greedily sucked one of Chuck's big juicy balls into their mouth. They sucked his balls good and hard, applying pressure to them with their lips and tongues.

"Ohhhhhhrrrr yeah," Chuck crooned breathlessly.

He put his hands back up behind his head and stood there real sexy looking in just his sneakers and socks as Dennis and Rodd feasted on him and feasted on him.

"Ohhhhhh yeah, suck my big sweaty balls you fuckers," Chuck crooned throatily.

As Dennis and Rodd did just that, sucked on the sexy bartender's balls I stood outside the bathroom keeping watch. No one was around. I pulled Chuck's shorts out of my pocket and pressed the crotch section of them to my nose and mouth. This time I was able to really get a nose full. They smelled of man sweat, sexy and hot. I gave the shorts a lick and then stuffed them back into my pocket. By now Dennis had Chuck's big hard cock in his mouth. He was sucking it like crazy, like his life depended on it while Chuck still stood with his hands crossed up behind his head, looking real submissive. Rodd was standing next to the stripped bartender and was licking one of his sweaty armpits and squeezing his big biceps at the same time.

"Ohhhhhrrrr yeah, getting real close now," Chuck crooned.

He swiveled his sexy hips in a seductive motion as Dennis ran his hands up and down his muscular thighs as he sucked and sucked his meat stick. Moments later, Chuck cried out that he was cumming. Dennis quickly took the beefy bartender's cock out of his mouth, grabbed it in his hand, and held it tightly and stroked it as Chuck shot his creamy load all over his massive chest.

"Ohhhhh yeah, yeah, fucking A!" Chuck crooned in total ecstasy as his sexy mess splattered all over him.

When he was done Dennis let go of the guy's cock and he and Rodd quickly began lapping the cum off Chuck's chest, paying special attention to his nipples, again sucking and slurping on them like crazy.

"Ohhhhh man, my fucking tits are all sensitive after I pop a load you guys, but what the fuck choice do I have here?" Chuck said breathlessly, gasping his words. "Have to let you two fucking horny bastards keep working me over till your shorts-stealing buddy gets back here. Oh yeah, suck my cum off my nips you fuckers! Gulp down my good stuff…"

Obviously the bartender was really into it all at that point…

Chuck closed his eyes and reeled in ecstasy as Dennis and Rodd slurped the cum off his nipples with real gusto. He shivered and shuddered as chills coursed through his magnificently muscular body. Just then, at that moment I walked into the bathroom. I saw that Chuck's cock was semi hard, with a bead of cum dangling off it from earlier. I walked over to him. As the bathroom door slammed shut Chuck opened his eyes, just in time to see me drop to my knees in front of him and slurp his big beefy cock into my mouth.

"Ohhhhhrrrrr!" Chuck groaned as I began earnestly sucking his big shaft. "Well, well. Look who the fuck is here, it's your shorts stealing buddy."

"Relax Dude," Dennis said to Chuck. "Just let him get you off again and then you might get your shorts back."

Chuck stayed in his stance with his hands up behind his head as I sucked his cock and Dennis and Rodd continued licking the cum from his big chest and sucking at his nipples in between.

"Fucker stole my shorts right off me just so he could chow down big and hearty on my meat," Chuck garbled breathlessly.

As I sucked Chuck's cock I saw Dennis and Rodd take their big cocks out of the fly openings in their jeans. They were both hard as rocks and pulsing. Working Chuck over sexually had gotten my two buddies real fucking horny. They jacked off onto Chuck's big chest, shooting their loads high and thick and then proceeded to lick that cum off the muscle boy also.

"Oh yeah you two, lick my goddamned muscle chest, eat my fucking tits," Chuck panted demandingly.

Then, Chuck grunted that he was about to shoot a second load. He grabbed me hard by the back of my neck and forced his big meat into my throat.

"Yeah, swallow my jizz you fucking shorts thief!" Chuck yelled, holding me tight by the back of my neck.

Dennis and Rodd each packed their cocks back into their jeans. My face was pressed right up against chuck's pubic bush and I was able to smell the piss that had landed there when I had tackled the big guy earlier.

"Yeah Howard, eat that hunky bartender's creamy load," Dennis said as he and Rodd left the bathroom.

When Chuck was done spewing his load he let his flaccid cock slip slowly out of my mouth and he stood towering over me in his muscular naked magnificence.

"Where are my damned shorts you bastard?" he asked me angrily.

I took Chuck's shorts out of my pocket and slid them over his sneaker and sweat socked feet, putting them back on him. Still on my knees I pressed my face against his crotch and gave it a kiss. I stood up and then gave each of his well-sucked nipples a kiss.

"It was just a joke," I said softly. "They dared me to do it."

Chuck pulled me close to himself and held me tight. I hugged him back, holding him tight also.

"I know," he said and squeezed my ass real hard. "I'm just glad you gave me back my shorts so that I can get back to work bud. When I get off work tonight I'll give them to you after I put my jeans on."

I slid to my knees again and licked his belly button, making my wish from earlier come true. Chuck shuddered involuntarily as my tongue burrowed deep in his belly button. Then, I stood up and exited the bathroom, leaving Chuck alone to finish his break.

Later, Dennis, Rodd and I were back sitting at the bar when Chuck returned.

"Hey, what took you so long?" the other bartender asked Chuck. "That was a long break."

"You wouldn't believe it if I told you," Chuck responded, looking over at the three of us with a sly smile on his handsome and beguiling face.

■

Captured Body Builder

"Ohhhhhrrr man," I moaned, groaned and swooned as yet another fucking guy slid his tongue up into my gaping and exposed ass hole. *"Fucking hole munchers…"*

His tongue flicked around in there like crazy, driving me totally batty. When he pressed his lips against the walls of my hole and began sucking it I thought I would literally fly away… I had lost count of how many guys had eaten, slurped, tongued, and sucked at my ass hole that night. I wondered how many of them had come back for second and third helpings of my very moist, very eaten ass hole. What I did know was that I was going no where anytime soon. I was in a slumped over position with my legs spread wide and tied tightly to a strange sort of table. My wrists were tightly bound in front of me with mounds of rope. (Fuckers had better have tied me tightly as I'm a pro body builder, fuckin' work out every day of the damned week for at least four to five hours a day.) My muscular and well-toned upper body was lashed to the table. Rope had been tied over my lean thighs and each of my long and wiry spread legs to hold them in place. And believe it or not rope had been tied around the sides of each of my big and round ass cheeks to hold them spread out so the men eating my hole didn't have to bother holding them spread themselves. Damn, but my cheeks sure felt numb and sore to put it bluntly. A cloth blindfold was tied over my eyes so I had no idea who the men were who were feasting repeatedly and over and over on my hole, and to make my situation that much worse, I had no fucking idea where I was.

"Arrrrhhhh *GAWD,*" I croaked as the fucking guy really went to town chowing on my damned hole. "Goddamn…"

Stinging slaps were delivered repeatedly to my spread out butt cheeks by a couple of the other men as the one eating me slurped and sucked and slurped and sucked. My big meaty and beefy dick was dangling long and semi hard between my legs, pulled through a large hole that had been cut into the table I was so thoroughly lashed to. My plum sized balls hung down along with the big guy, a rope tied just around the top of them. For the moment they were leaving my dick and balls alone but earlier they too had been sucked and slurped like mad. I had been made to shoot my load numerous times and *fuck,* but hadn't it drove me utterly crazy when that guy had kept sucking the tip of my dick after I had shot that third creamy load. The guy eating my hole took a few last sucks at it and then stopped. He stuck a finger deep in there and I heard the sound of men chuckling. God, I imagined them all standing around the table, looking over the helpless and bound and blindfolded bodybuilder, stripped to his damned gray colored silk calf length dress socks and feasting away at his very wet hole. Suddenly, I felt the awful sting of the leather paddles on my butt cheeks, again.

"Awwwwrr no no," I roared miserably and struggled like crazy to get untied. "Not again you bastards, don't fuckin' beat my poor cheeks again."

They rapped my butt cheeks harder and harder with each stroke of the leather paddles, tenderizing the poor big and round guys, really putting the screws to them. This was actually the third time I was being given a hard, painful, and stinging paddling. I wondered if I would cry as hard as I did with the earlier spanking I had been dealt.

"Ayyyyrrrrr…" I screamed, as the blows became harder and harder and more intense with each blow.

As my butt cheeks were being beaten I felt the sticky and sweet honey that had been poured into my hole earlier being slopped onto my fingers with some sort of a basting brush.

"Ayyyyrrrr GAWDS," I grunted. "What now you stinking fuckers?"

As my butt cheeks were beaten harder and harder I felt my fingers suddenly being sucked like dicks, one by one. Admittedly, it felt awesome as the guy teased the tips of my honey soaked fingers with the tip of his tongue. (If you've never had someone suck at your fingers like that give it a try, you won't regret it.) My dick grew hard under the table and my poor balls ached from the rope tied around them. Even while my butt cheeks were being beaten my damned dick grew hard, *shit!* After I don't know how many harsh and stinging blows to my butt cheeks with the leather paddles, they finally stopped rapping me. Tears of anger and fear soaked my blindfold. One of the guys scurried under the table and slurped my big Spanish dick into his mouth and sucked it for all he was worth as his buddy went on sucking at my fingers. I felt a tongue slide up into my very exposed hole and I nearly spun away. Okay, one of them was sucking my fingers, one of them was sucking my dick, and one of them was *again* eating my hole. That made three guys, but there were more of them, I could sense it. *I knew there were more of them!*

"Fucking guys man," I gasped. "Why the fuck are you doin' this to me?"

Fingers gripped one of my ass cheeks hard and I heard mean and fiendish chuckling. I pursed my lips as I felt myself getting close to shooing another load of creamy eggnog for them to chow down on. As I was about to cum I tried to think back to how the evening had begun, and how I had managed to come to be in this more than fucked up position.

It was a Friday night. The workweek was over. I had decided to have a few cold beers at a bar in my neighborhood that was called The Local before going to sleep that night. Also, one never knows whom one might meet at The Local, if you catch my drift. And, being that it was the night before my birthday I felt I deserved to treat myself to a few beers. So, I shucked off my scuffed work boots, my worn jeans, my sweat soaked tee shirt, and my stinking briefs and sweat socks and walked naked to the bathroom to shower before heading out to The Local. I stunk like a foot ball player's locker room after a big game in the heat. My job as a construction worker helps to keep me in the finest shape possible. As the warm water cascaded over my well-built muscular body I soaped myself up, lathering up my firm biceps and arms, running soapy fingers over my huge chest. I gave my nipples a squeeze each and my dick jutted out in front of me, long, hard, and pulsing. My balls hung down nice and plump. I squeezed one of my nipples again, and with a soapy hand I grabbed my big beefy guy. Smiling, standing there under the warm water as it flowed over me, relaxing my very worked muscles, I stroked my guy slowly.

"Ohhhh yeah," I moaned, my voice echoing in the tile bathroom.

With one hand teasing one of my now erect nipples and the other stroking my dick, I slowly led myself to orgasm. I love popping my load, love seeing that creamy load of ball juice erupt from my big dick slit, and at the age of twenty four I have no problem getting myself off more than a few times before the day is out. Fuck, I figured that even if I did meet someone tonight at The Local I would still have plenty of jizz to feed the fucker after shooting my eggnog in the shower.

"Ohhhhrr yeah," I grunted. "Fuckin' A…"

I let go of my nipple, grabbed my balls, and squeezed them gently as I let fly with a big load of Spanish boy spunk.

"Arrrrrhhh yeahh yeah," I grunted wildly as I stood there with one hand stroking my big dick and the other hand hefting my balls as I drained them.

When I was done I let the water massage my body a little more and then turned off the water. I stepped out of the shower, towel dried, and padded to the bathroom to get dressed. I pulled on a pair of fresh white briefs, gray silk calf length dress socks, a pair of charcoal colored jeans, a black tank top, a cotton black summer jacket, and a pair of black highly shined ankle length boots. I rolled the sleeves up on my jacket, got my wallet and keys, and feeling really good left the apartment. The Local is a little more than twenty blocks from my apartment, and being that it was a cool summer evening I decided to walk there, rather than take the bus. When I walked into The Local the place was somewhat crowded with the usual crowd of neighborhood guys, some guys cruising, and some who were there just for a drink before heading home after working overtime. Suits, construction workers, and everything in between came to The Local to kick back and relax. The smell of alcohol and cigarette smoke greeted me as I walked through the place and up to the big bar. The Local is a pretty big place for a neighborhood bar, dimly lit with lots of neon signs advertising different brands of beer. A pool table adorns the back end of the bar and I saw a few guys in Levi's and tee shirts playing a game of pool back there. I wondered what they were playing for tonight. A fast grin past over my face at that thought. Off to the side and down a short hallway was the men's room. I've had my tube steak sucked more than a few times in that men's room when I didn't feel like bringing the guy back to my apartment and having him spends the night with me. There's a stall in there with a big Old Glory hole cut into it for guys who are into that shit. One time a while back a guy sucked me for all he was worth as I stood in that stall with my pants and briefs down around my ankles and my dick and balls sticking through the glory hole. Fucking guy sucked my stinking and sweaty dick and balls real good let me tell you. I had come into the bar right after working all day in the grueling sun and I smelled all ripe and funky. As he sucked me his hands moved over and over the exposed black dress socks I happened to be wearing that day. In between sucking me he commented on how kinky it was that I happened to be wearing suit socks with my construction clothes. I breathlessly told him how all my sweat socks were in the laundry and I was forced to wear the dress socks that day. After the fucking guy managed to suck two hefty loads of ball juice out of me he begged me to let him have the black dress socks I was wearing as I stood there in front of the stall, packing my well sucked dick and balls back into my jeans.

"Fuck man, you are a kinky dude," I said with a grin.

So, I leaned up against a sink, unlaced my boots, and shucked them off. The guy squatted in front of me and slid my black socks off my feet. He stood up, rolled the socks tight, and took a hearty sniff of them, as I stood there bare footed. I smiled from ear to ear.

"Thanks guy," he said, patted my crotch, and exited the men's room with my socks.

"Next time you can have my briefs too," I thought as I slipped my bare and stinking feet into my boots.

As I walked up to the bar I looked down the hallway at the men's room and saw a couple of guys going in there. To piss or to fool around I did not know.

"Hey Eddie," the bartender, a handsome guy named Clyde said to me as I came up to the bar. "What'll it be guy?"

"Hi Clyde," I said and shook hands with him. "Give me a twenty ounce Bud, a real cold one."

"Coming up Eddie," Clyde said and placed a can of Budweiser and a cold mug in front of me on the bar.

I handed him a ten-dollar bill and he placed the change in front of me on the bar. I poured beer into the mug and took a long hearty gulp of it.

"So, how are things?" Clyde asked me, his eyes looking hungrily at my chest area just visible over my tank top.

"Work is busy and tomorrow I'm celebrating my twenty fifth birthday Clyde my man," I said and held up my mug of beer.

"Hey, good for you man, happy b-day," Clyde said. "Next one is on the house Eddie."

"Thanks Clyde," I replied with a smile and took another gulp of my beer.

I put the beer down, shucked off my jacket, and held it under my arm as I stood at the bar. I felt eyes devouring me, looking at me hungrily and lustfully. Clyde placed a tall glass of Budweiser in front of me on the bar alongside my half empty can.

"There ya go Eddie, happy b-day again man on the house," Clyde said and rushed off to serve another waiting patron.

I finished my first beer, smiled, and took a long sip of the second one. It was horribly warm and tasty like piss.

"Holy shit," I whispered and looked in Clyde's direction, wanting to ask for a better glass of beer.

He saw me looking at him and smiled over at me. I held up the glass of piss tasting beer, stupidly took another sip, and grimaced. Clyde smiled at the silly look on my face. Now, as I lay tied to the table and about to shoot a fourth (fifth, sixth? I had lost count) load of eggnog for the kidnappers who had me trapped I had small flashes of memory. I placed the glass of warm piss tasting beer on the bar and my head spun. I was suddenly very dizzy and in need of a seat. I grabbed the side of the bar and I heard a voice from somewhere far away asking me if I was okay, saying that I didn't look that good at the moment. Then, fingers toying with and twisting one of my big nipples under my tank top as my vision blurred. The glass of warm piss tasting beer was held to my lips and I heard another voice telling me to drink up, that it would help me feel better in no time. I wanted to tell whoever it was that the beer was awful and that I didn't want to drink it. I was force fed the beer and I felt a hand gripping one of my butt cheeks.

"Ohhhhrrrr shit," I gasped as I shot my load into the guy's mouth that was sucking me. "Fucking bastards, guys drugged me. That's how you managed to snag me."

When I was done cumming the guy at my dick slurped one of my testicles into his mouth and applied pressure to it with his tongue.

"Ayyyyrrrr!" I roared angrily.

The guy at my fingers had two of my fingers in his mouth at the moment and the guy at my ass was slurping wildly and madly at my hole.

"Fucking kidnappers, drugged my damned beer," I rasped miserably.

The guy eating my hole stopped and suddenly my butt cheeks were *again* being pummeled with the leather paddles.

"Owwwrrrr no, no," I yelled madly. "Not this shit again you fuckers!"

My butt cheeks were beyond hurting at that point, they were stinging and burning with the pain. As they beat my cheeks and the guys sucked my balls and my fingers my mind drifted again, back to The Local. When the glass of awful tasting beer was empty (they had made me drink it all) I could barely stand up.

"Oh man, you are in bad shape mister," I heard a voice say to me from somewhere very far away.

My vision was totally blurred. All I saw were blurred images of the neon signs around the bar.

"Maybe we should get him outside so he can get some air," another far away voice said.

Hands grabbed my wrists and pulled my hands off the end of the bar as I gripped it for dear life.

"N-no, can't," I whispered and they slung my arms across their shoulders.

"Is he okay?" I heard someone ask, I think it was Clyde.

"Just had a little too much to drink," I heard someone reply. "Big guy like him you would think he could drink like a fish."

They moved me slowly across and out of the bar. The image faded again though as the fuckers really beat the tar out of my butt cheeks.

"Okay, that's enough," I heard one of the men say. "Anymore and the poor fuck will wind up bleeding all over the place."

They stopped paddling me. It was the first time I had heard any of them speak since this had all began. I was whimpering like a child and crying big tears behind my blindfold. The guy under the table now had my dick back in his mouth and was sucking it all over again. Actually, for all I knew it could have been one of the other guys down there taking a turn at my big Spanish sausage. My balls were hanging low and pulsing miserably with pain, and the other guy was still sucking my damned fingers.

"Get him a drink," I heard that voice say again. "He needs to calm down."

At the sound of those words my heart leapt with terror in my big chest. Then, I felt a glass being placed to my trembling lips. I clamped my mouth shut, knowing it was the drugged beer I had been given at the bar.

"He won't drink it," I heard another say.

"Not a problem," the first voice said merrily. "There's another way we can make him drink it."

I felt a plastic tube being slid into my exposed ass hole and then the beer was being poured through it and into my gut. They had slid a damned household funnel into my hole.

"Oh shiiiiiittttt!" I screeched and my head spun as it did back at the bar.

If I wasn't blindfolded I was sure my vision would have blurred as well.

My hole literally sucked up and drank the warm drugged beer, as I lay there totally helpless to stop these men from using me as a suck-on toy. Unbelievably I felt myself getting ready to shoot my eggnog again. My head hit the table and more images appeared to me. Outside The Local, I was being half walked half carried through a parking lot and over to a big van.

"Wh-whassss goin' on?" I slurred. "Wh-whaaa you g-guys thin-think you're doin'?"

I sounded totally stupid and totally drunk. Then, the back doors of the van were open and everything went black as I felt the cloth being tied over my eyes. They hoisted me into the van, keeping my hands behind me now, not wanting me to reach up and get the blindfold off. Then, my clothes being taken off me ripped off me too. They tore my tank top off me, hands pulled my boots off my feet, and my jeans were yanked down and off me. My briefs were torn off me and I was held propped against a wall of the van as hands explored and squeezed me everywhere. My nipples were sucked and licked like crazy as was my dick and balls as I stood there wearing just my silk gray dress socks. I was so out of it by then that I could not speak at all. My lips felt like they were twice their size. I think I shot a load for them in the van, and I think the guy sucking me swallowed it. Greedy fucks, they had swallowed every shot they had sucked out of me thus far. Then, they tied me in a hog-tied position on the floor of the van. I heard a couple of the guys get out of the van, the back doors slammed shut, and the van started moving. I guessed that the guys who had gotten out were riding up front while the others stayed in the back with me.

"Man, are you in for some real fun," I heard a voice say from inside my head and then I felt tongues licking the bottoms of my silk socked feet.

Now, the fuckers had me shooting yet another load of cream for them. As the guy sucking my dick swallowed every drop of it I moaned softly and miserably. The funnel had been taken out of my sopping wet hole and when I was done cumming the guy let my dick slip out of his mouth.

"Let's clean this hole of his before eating it again," I heard that echoed voice say. "We don't want to accidentally drink any of the beer we gave him."

I heard chuckling and then an ice cube was pressed against my hole.

"Ohhhh no, no, not this again," I rasped more to myself than out loud.

They slid the ice cube all over my hole, their fingers prodding it in between the cleaning it was getting. I shivered from the cold under the tight and binding ropes as the ice cube was run over my exposed and very eaten hole. The guy had stopped sucking my fingers, as there was no more honey on them for him to suck. But then, when my hole was spic and span clean I felt the sticky honey being slopped in there and again my hole was being feasted upon.

"Fuck," I whispered. "Honeyed up my hole again eh? Bet it tastes real good back there…"

As the guy slurped and sucked my hole again my mind again drifted to how all this had begun. I suddenly recalled the van I was hog-tied in coming to a stop. The back doors opened and I heard the men chuckling mockingly.

"Shit, look at you guys, licking his damned feet," one of the guys who had been up front said laughingly. "How do those socks of his taste huh?"

"Can't fucking leave him alone man," one of the men sucking my socked toes said and snapped the elastic in one of my socks against my calf.

"Well come on, let's get him inside," I heard the first voice say.

Then, I was being lifted and carried out of the van. I guessed that we were in a garage that was connected to a house. That was the only way they could get me from the van to the house totally unseen. I mean most people who happened to see a bound, blindfolded guy wearing just his socks being carted into a house by a group of kidnappers would most surely call the police. And to carry a body builder as heavily muscled as I there had to be more than three or four of the men. Once in the house they undid the hog-tie I was in but left me blindfolded as they proceeded to rope me to the table I was now on. I was still pretty woozy from the drugged beer I had drunk so I was not able to stop them from tying me securely to the table and spreading my legs wide. Before they started eating and slurping at my damned hole they each ran an ice cube against it, driving me crazy with the cold, cleaning me out back there with the cubes and what felt like paper towels. The way my dick and balls were hanging freely down under the table I knew that there had to be a large hole carved into it, just for that purpose.

"Wha-wha you guys want?" I asked in a drunken slur as they continued pressing ice cubes against my hole and delivering open handed slaps to my big bound ass cheeks.

I received no reply however, except more hard open handed slaps on my butt cheeks. When the ice cubes were melted down and too small they deposited what was left of them into my opened hole. I shivered madly at the cold and indecency of it.

"Fuckers, kidnapped me…" I whispered miserably.

When my hole was cleaned to their satisfaction I felt the first helping of the sticky and sweet honey being smeared in there with various fingers. They stuck their fingers into my hole as they slopped the honey in and out of it, preparing a treat for them. I then felt the first tongue lapping hungrily and maddeningly at my hole and I nearly jumped out of my skin. I yelped and goose bumps broke out all over me. Other tongues were licking and kissing my tied spread out ass cheeks and one of the guys went under the table to gobble my big sausage sized dick into his mouth. As I was sucked and licked I realized that they were treating me like a damned buffet. When all the honey had been licked out of my hole they smeared another good helping into it and took turns licking and sucking it out. The guy under the table went on sucking me until I shot a good hefty sized load of eggnog for him to swallow. He gulped down my juices, sucking at the tip of my dick only now, really making my head spin. When the second helping of honey was all eaten out of my hole I was given the first of various hard and painful stinging spankings with their leather paddles. As I was spanked hard and screaming in pain another guy found his way under the table, tugged my balls down low, tied a rope around the top of them, and slurped my semi hard dick into his eager cock sucking mouth.

"Ohhhhrrr shit, don't fuckin' suck me off again so soon you fuckers," I grunted as chills and pain coursed through me.

So there I was, a fuckin' muscle bound strong dude, totally helpless, tied down, blindfolded, stripped to my socks, and having my ass hole and cock repeatedly sucked. As I said earlier, I had no fucking idea where I was *or* who the men were that had me trapped in such a mortifying way. They were again taking turns licking and slurping at my hole and my head spun from the warm drugged beer that they had funneled in there.

"Ohhhhrrr GAWD," I moaned as I felt one of them under the table licking at the tip of my dick.

"Okay guys, let's get this boy off one more time and then we'll give him what he really needs," I heard the guy under the table say and then he slurped me into his mouth.

24

He sucked me to a new hard on as the other guys kept taking turns eating, licking, and slurping at my hole. My dick was feeling sore and numb at that point and it took quite a while before I shot a small spurt of eggnog for the cock sucker under the table to feast on, his tongue teasing my dick slit even after I had come.

"Ayyyrrrrr…" I grunted wildly as they drove me practically insane.

When I was done cumming for what felt like the umpteenth time the guy let my dick slip out of his mouth. I lay there huffing, heaving, and gasping for breath as they stopped eating my hole. I was a sweaty and stinking mess and feeling totally woozy and used up.

"Feelin' good?" one of the men asked me and gave my ass cheeks a squeeze each.

"Y-yeah, just great," I whimpered and managed to lift my head up off the table. *Just what I've always dreamed of, bein' kidnapped and treated like a buffet table at an all night party…"*

Suddenly, the blindfold was whisked off me and as my eyes adjusted to the light I looked up at my captors.

"Ho-holy shit!" I said loudly and a wicked smile came across my lips as relief filled me. "Oh holy fuck, you fucking guys!"

Looking up, I saw six of my work buddies from the job. Ron, Steve, Lenny, Kevin, Danny, and Angel were all standing around the table with their big dicks sticking out of their jeans.

"Happy birthday Eddie!" they said loudly in unison.

I laughed along with them, loving the birthday joke they had played on me. They must have recalled a conversation we'd had a while back where I mentioned what a sick thrill it would be for a guy to be kidnapped and used as a sex toy. Fucking guys saved it up for my birthday gift. They gave my ass a few hard slaps each and prodded my wet hole with their fingers.

"Fucking guys, best buddies a guy could ever have," I said with a grin on my face. "But was it really necessary to paddle the fuck out of my poor cheeks?"

"Just think of them as birthday paddles," Ron, the ringleader as always said and ruffled my dark hair.

Lenny tied the blindfold back on me and for the remainder of the party I had to guess which of them was fucking my very lubricated hole. For each wrong guess I was paddled again… Overall, it was actually the best fucking birthday party I ever had, a party that went on all fucking night as my buddies fucked the tar out of me, ate my hole again and again, and forced me to shoot still more gobs of Spanish eggnog for them.

Thanks guys…

■

The Captain of the Football Team

My name is Roger. With all the magazines that I see out there nowadays dealing with bondage, S&M, B&D, and other hot kinky issues I thought that I would share an experience I had years ago with you. Actually, it was an experience that I started out bearing witness to and thanks to a strange stroke of luck got to participate in as well. It was way back when I was in college. I had gone to school out of state so I lived in a dorm on campus. One afternoon I was in study hall reading up on my English notes, studying for an upcoming exam when I realized that I didn't have my English textbook. I nearly panicked but then remembered that I had left it in my gym locker. I stood up, gathered my other books under my arm, and proceeded to the gym locker room. The door was ajar so it made no sound when I pulled it the rest of the way open and walked in, leaving it slightly ajar after entering the locker room as well. Like most men's locker rooms it smelled of a mixture of male sweat, dirty socks, jocks and underwear and piss. As I approached my locker I suddenly heard the sound of someone moaning. The sound was coming from one of the rows of lockers in the back of the locker room. Being overly nosy I decided to investigate, but did not want to get caught. As I walked slowly on my sneaker feet toward the place where the moaning was coming from I was able to determine that it was a husky male voice that I was hearing. Whoever he was he was moaning and groaning in out-right passion. I figured that some lucky dude had snuck his girlfriend into the locker room to have some fun with her between classes and between her legs as well. I got closer and was able to hear his deep voice. He was saying things like, "Yeah, oh yeah, suck them, oh yeah, fucking A!" From his words of "suck them" I figured his girlfriend was polishing his nuts with her mouth and tongue. When I was around the corner from where the moaning was coming from I pressed myself up against a locker, wishing I could turn invisible. I peered around carefully and stealthily to see who the fuck was having so much fun. What I saw totally shocked me. Two guys who I had seen from time to time on campus had another dude stripped to his sweaty white underpants and white sweat socks. They had him pressed up against a locker and they were each sucking and slurping one of his nipples like their lives depended on it. Fuck, they were sucking his big nips like crazy. To add to my shock I saw that the guy who was having his nipples sucked like a lollipop was blindfolded *and* that his hands were securely roped behind his back at the wrists. As the two guys continued to suck and slurp his nipples relentlessly I realized that the blindfolded tied up dude was the college football team's captain. Fuck, somehow or other these two guys had managed to ambush the handsome and rugged football dude, get him tied up and blindfolded and were now working him over. (If you call having your big man tits sucked and slurped worked over that is.) As I watched (totally transfixed) the football team's captain's dick was getting hard as a rock in his sweaty briefs. The way the guy was sopped and glistening with sweat I figured that they'd been at it for some time at that point. The football dude's underpants were practically stuck to his skin. Even from where I was standing I was able to see the big meaty bulge pressing against the white cotton sweaty soaked material of his underpants. It was throbbing in there, begging for release. One of the guys kneeled down, pulled the football team's captain's meaty dick out of the fly opening in his briefs, and gobbled the giant piece of meat into his mouth. I nearly gasped. The other guy continued sucking and slurping on the captain's nipple that was in his mouth.

"Oh yeah, suck my dick you fucker!" the football team captain groaned and slid his sweat slicked body up and down against the metal locker he was propped up against.

He was looking up, seeing nothing but his thoughts as one of the men sucked and slurped one of his nipples and the other guy sucked his big meat like crazy. He struggled fruitlessly to get his hands untied, his big muscles flexing in his over-sized arms with the effort. Although with what the two guys were doing to him I doubted very much he wanted to get free at all. The football team's captain was a buzz-cut blond fellow, muscular and well toned, (built like a brick shit house to put it plainly) and smooth and hairless everywhere on his more than magnificent body. Besides football he worked out on a regular basis. He had attested to that in a college newspaper interview. He was writhing more and more in ecstasy against the locker he was pressed up against as the two men (both of them dressed in jeans, pullover shirts, and sneakers) sucked him harder and harder.

"Fuckers, you didn't need to fucking tie me up *and* blindfold me for this shit," the team captain swore breathlessly. "Fuck it all, I would have let you faggots suck my dick and nips any fucking time. Feels better than when my damned girlfriend does it to me…"

"You look hotter this way Captain," one of the men said and quickly resumed sucking the football team's captain.

"Yeah, bet I do at that," the captain mumbled, a sinister looking grin crossing his handsome blindfolded face.

Standing there watching I felt rooted to the spot. My dick was hard and more than throbbing in my jeans, and I was sweating like crazy. As my hands sweated I didn't realize that one of my hard covered books was slipping out of my hand. The book suddenly hit the floor with a loud sounding thud. I quickly moved behind the locker I was peering around, out of sight.

"What the fuck was that?" one of the guys asked, sounding nervous.

"I don't know," his buddy replied just as nervously.

Obviously they had stopped sucking on the football captain.

"Come on man, lets get the fuck out of here," the first guy said. "I don't feel like getting caught like this!"

As they hightailed it out the back door I peered slowly around the corner again. The football team's captain was still standing there, tied and blindfolded, *totally helpless.*

"Hey!" the captain roared angrily. *"Get back here you two! Don't leave me here like this! Shit!"*

I heard the back door to the locker room slam shit and realized that I was now alone with the football team's captain. I took a deep breath, and silently walked over to him.

"*Fuck, fuck, fuck,*" the football captain was muttering more than angrily.

He was standing there, struggling for real now to get his hands untied. I stepped closer to him till I was just a few feet from him. I put my books silently down on the floor and walked closer to him still. He looked more than beyond sexy the way he was standing there, a look of total helplessness etched on his handsome blindfolded face. Stripped to his socks and underpants, tied and blindfolded, smelling real funky and ripe and with his big throbbing meat sticking out of his under shorts the football captain looked like a feast fit for a king.

"Who's there?" he suddenly barked angrily. "Fuck, I know someone is there. Look, it was all part of a joke; I'm not a faggot or anything like that. We were all just having some fun here. Please, untie me and take this damned blindfold off me. I assure you man, this wasn't all my idea..."

I stepped closer to him till I was standing nose to nose with him, till I could smell his breath on my face. He was so much bigger than I. He could easily break me in half, if his hands weren't tightly tied behind him that is. Fuck man, the guy was as strong as an ox and built like an iron man. My breath was coming in gasps and I silently thanked my lucky stars for this chance experience.

"Look, I know someone is here," he went on, not knowing that I was standing directly in front of him. "I can fuckin' hear you breathing. Gads, sounds like you're in love with me or something bud."

I leaned down, slurped one of his overly erect nipples into my mouth, and began sucking on it.

"Ohhhhhhhhh fuck, *what the hell?*" he gasped in utter disbelief.

The tip of his nipple was hard as a fucking bullet and more than erect as my tongue slid over it and my lips sucked on it. Holding him by his hips I pulled him away from the locker he was leaning against. Slowly and reluctantly he moved toward me on his socked feet as I continued slurping and sucking the fuck out of his nipple.

"Oh gads, stop this, *stop this shit now!*" he pleaded. "Th-this was all a game between me and just those two other guys. I-I don't know who the fuck you are man, but no one fucking invited you! *Ohhhhhhhrrr fuck...*"

He managed to balance himself on his wobbly socked feet as I held him tightly by his hips, sucking and slurping his nipples alternately till they were red and even more erect. I held him tighter and tighter as I tongue bathed his sore nipples.

"Fucking bastard, whoever the fuck you are," the football captain swore. *"Fucking eating and feasting on my damned tits must be lunch time for you or something man, seeing as you think I'm a goddamned buffet!"*

To shut him up I pressed my lips against his and kissed him hard on the mouth. Surprisingly, his tongue darted into my mouth and explored it. He really loved every second of this, despite the way he was bitching and complaining. I decided to give him more, see just how far I could push the big football guy. I took a step back away from him and ran my hands all over his tits, his pecs, his stomach area, his broader than broad shoulders and squeezed his biceps and sore nipples, twisting them a few times rather meanly.

"Easy with my nips you fucker," he said threateningly, even though he knew there wasn't anything he could do to me at the moment.

I squeezed and twisted his nipples harder, inflicting a little pain.

"Uhhhhhh…" he moaned.

His meat stick was *still* hard as a fucking rock while sticking out of his briefs. It was by now more than oozing droplets and big beads of pre cum, waiting to shoot a hefty load or two. God knows the guy was big enough to get off a few fucking times. Holding the big lug by his upper arms I moved him further still away from the locker and got him balanced on his socked and wobbly feet. I stepped behind the football team captain and wrapped my arms tightly around him, pulled him close to me, ran my hands over his tits, and again and again squeezed and twisted them hard.

"Ohhhhhhrrrr God, please, *please let me see who the fuck you are man,"* he pleaded desperately. "Please, take this blindfold off and let me see you…"

I noticed however that he wasn't asking to be untied. My dick was hard in my pants as I rubbed it against his rear end…

Moments later I had the football team captain sitting on the bench between the rows of lockers as I knelt before him sucking his giant meat. I had taken his briefs off him, stuffed them in a pocket of my jeans to keep as a souvenir of this experience, and guided him by his muscular rock hard arms to a sitting position on the bench. His dick was beyond huge to say the least. I sucked it like crazy, having to force it to the back of my mouth, pressing my nose against the spot where his Very light bush of pubic hair was. I inhaled the scent of his pubic hair as I played suck with his meat stick. I gave his big sweat smelling balls a tongue bath and then resumed sucking the fuck out of his dick.

"Ohhhhhhh man, you are driving me fucking crazy, whoever the fuck you are," the football team captain said breathlessly.

He leaned back on the bench, his tightly bound hands pressed against the wood.

"Ohhhh yeah, suck my meat you bastard," he groaned. "Chow down on that tube steak of mine!"

He thrust in and out of my mouth, making me eat the droplets of pre cum that were oozing from his wide sexy slit.

"Ohhhhhhrrrrr God, I-I'm goin' to shoot man," the football captain grumbled. "I'm goin' to fuckin' shoot my damned load!"

He shot a load big enough to choke a horse. I swallowed some of it, just to get a real good taste of the giant fucking guy, and let the rest of it squirt over his big muscular chest, creating a feast for me. I held his throbbing boner tightly in my hand, as he seemed to go on and on spurting giant globs of his thick cream onto his chest.

"Arrrrrrrrhhhhh fuck, got me cumming like a bitch in heat on a hot Saturday night man," the football captain panted.

He was leaning even further back now, all stretched out, moaning and swearing like a fucking captured marine all the while. He grimaced in seething pleasure behind his blindfold as I squeezed more and more of the good stuff from him. When he was finally done and thoroughly soaked with his own football jizz I slowly let go of his dick, giving it a few last squeezes as I did so, getting some real shudders out of him. He sat there panting and breathing heavily. I wondered is he always shot such hefty loads or if it what was happening to him at the moment that had him so unusually excited. As he was about to sit up I pressed a hand against his chest and pushed him backward, stretching the guy out on the bench. With some rope I found nearby on the floor (no doubt it had been left there by the two guys that I had found the football captain with) I had tied his socked feet and his big arms to the bench, securing the big side of beef to it. As he lay there totally helpless I slowly ran the tip of my tongue over his chest, licking up his cum.

"Ohhhhh man, *I really wish* you would let me see who the fuck you are man," he pleaded arrogantly. "Fuck man, never had a guy eat my mess before. Fuck, fuck, this shit feels great, and I'm not even a faggot!"

His body rocked up and down on the bench as I sucked his cum off his nipples, really putting the screws to them.

"Ohhhhhrrrrr Fucker, sucking and eating my poor sore tits," he grumbled miserably.

When I had finished licking just about all the cum off his chest I saw that his meat stick had gotten hard again. I grabbed it in hand, stroked him up to a new throbbing boner and forced him to cum a second time, shooting another hefty sized load of football cream onto his muscular smooth chest.

"Ohhhhhhhrrrr shit, shit! *You fucking bastard, whoever you are,"* he ranted. "One helping wasn't enough for you huh? Had to make me cook up another batch of my hot jizz for you! Ohhhhhhrrr God man, my nuts are churning, got me shooting like goddamned gangbusters!"

As I again licked his cum off his chest I squeezed his nipples hard, making him yell out in a mixture of pain and pleasure all at once. Like most guys his nipples were pretty sensitive after he'd shot his load. When I was done licking his cum off him the second time I looked down at him and my heart more than accelerated in my chest. He really was a work of art, muscles everywhere, so finely toned, not an ounce of fat on him and looking so helpless tied and blindfolded, sopped in his sweat and remnants of cum. Beads of piss pearled at his slit. Slowly, I pulled my hard dick out of my jeans and began stroking myself, aiming at his big muscular chest.

"Wh-what are you doin' man?" he asked me when he didn't feel me messing with him. "Look, untie me, don't fuckin' leave me here like this like those two ass holes did. There's going to be a class coming in here soon. Imagine how those dudes will react to seeing the college football captain all trussed up in his socks and under shorts."

"Then I guess I had better hurry," I said to myself.

"Fuck man, I can hear you strokin' bud, you're jack in' off huh?" he barked. "Fucking faggot, getting off on seeing a big jock like me all trussed up, *shit! Today sure as fuck is your lucky day bud."*

I shot my load all over his chest and he reeled in anger and ecstasy all over again as I licked it off him, torturing his nipples with my mouth, sucking on them like crazy, nipping them, savoring the taste of them. After we were both spent I packed my semi hardness back into my jeans and untied him from the bench, leaving his hands tied behind him and the blindfold on him. I helped him to a sitting position and sat down next to him on the bench. Holding his giant arms in a firm grasp I kissed him hard on the mouth. Again he responded by darting his tongue deeply into my mouth and moving it around in there.

"I'm keeping your briefs," I whispered softly in his ear.

"Keep them," he said miserably. "You can even have my damned smelly socks too! Just please untie me."

Smiling, I reached down and pulled his sweat socks off his feet. The smell of his big sweaty feet assaulted my nostrils, and had there been time I would have stretched the big lug out on the bench again and licked the fuck out of his rancid feet.

"Shit, I wasn't being literal Fucker!" he yelled. "Fucking pervert, stealing my damned under shorts and socks…"

I loosened the ropes around his wrists just a little and then quickly walked away from him, taking my books with me. I watched from around the corner as he sat there slowly working his hands free, his meat stick growing hard again. He grunted and swore angrily with the effort, sweating like crazy, naked as the day he was born.

"UHHHRRRRR!" he ranted through clenched teeth as he worked his hands free.

But then, what I thought would happen, did. The two guys who had been working the football team captain over earlier came back. When they saw him struggling, his hands just about free they smirked meanly at each other. They walked quickly over to the football captain and pulled him to his feet by his muscular upper arms.

"Unnnnffff!" the captain grunted in surprise as they hoisted him up off the bench.

"Hey Captain my Captain, where are your briefs and socks?" the first guy asked him mockingly, giving one of his nipples a tight squeeze and jiggle.

"Yeah, and why the fuck are you untying your hands?" the second guy asked him just as mockingly. "We are far from done with you big guy."

The second guy quickly resecured the ropes around the football team captain's wrists.

"No, no, *oh no, untie me already you fuckers!*" the football team captain pleaded miserably. "Someone was in here and he took my fuckin' under shorts and socks. He worked me over guys, made me cum two fucking times. Just look at my damned tits. Fucking guy, whoever he was ate them up like crazy. They must be red and sore as hell!"

"Yep, they sure as shit are Captain," the first guy said, tweaking the captain's other nipple real hard.

"Fucking dude, whoever he was, he even kissed me," the football captain said despondently. "Goddamned faggot I was in the clutches of."

"C'mon, lets fucking put him in that giant duffel bag the team uses for game supplies and carry this side of beef to our dorm room," the first guy said. "There's going to be a class coming in here soon and I don't feel like sharing this giant stud with anybody else today."

"You're on," the second guy said. "But we'd better find something to gag him with as well. Don't want him yelling and swearing while we're lugging him across campus in the duffel bag."

Together, they hoisted the football team captain off the floor and carried him away.

"Fuckers, put me down," I heard the captain ranting as they walked off with him.

Anyway, that was many years ago at this point. A few times during my years at college there I past the captain of the football team in the halls and outside the college as well. He never found out that I was the guy who had worked him over, feasted on his cum, kissed him and taken his briefs and socks as souvenirs in the locker room that day. To him I was just another guy passing in the hallways and outside on campus. Till this day I have those briefs and socks of his. I have never washed them, sleazy fucker that I am…

■

The Plumber

When I was nineteen years old I had one of my first gay sexual experiences, in my parent's house of all places. I was still living at home but had long ago realized that I was gay. It was during the month of July and the New York heat was intense and overwhelming. It was a Wednesday afternoon, my day off from work. The sink in the kitchen was stopped up and my parents had asked me to stay home to let the plumber in when he got there. They both had to work so I agreed to stay home that day. The plumber had said that he would be at our house any time between eight A.M and twelve P.M. I had only heard his voice on the phone but I expected him to look like all plumbers I had seen before, a guy with a potbelly, gray hair, and old. At ten A.M. the doorbell rang. Dressed in blue shorts, sneakers with no socks, and a white tee shirt I opened the door.

"Hi," the plumber said. "I'm here to fix the sink."

At the sight of him my breath caught in my throat. He was beyond handsome; he was beyond good looking. He was *fucking gorgeous*.

"Sure, come in," I replied, holding the door open for him.

He looked to be about six feet tall. He had jet-black hair, dark eyes, (like two black marbles in his head) and no facial hair whatsoever. I could tell that he was extremely muscular from the way his chest was pressing against his tee shirt. He was wearing olive green work pants, a black tight fitting tee shirt with his company logo printed on the breast pocket of it, and scuffed up black construction boots. He was carrying a large toolbox in one hand. I guessed his age to be mid to late twenties.

"So, where's the culprit?" he asked me with a big smile.

My heart was thundering wildly in my chest. He had a smile that could melt anyone's heart.

"This way," I said, walking toward the kitchen.

As he walked behind me my legs felt weak and my knees felt like they had turned to rubber. In the kitchen I pointed to the sink. I explained how the water would not drain and that my father had had to use a bucket to get all the stopped up water out of the sink the night before.

"Hmmm…" the plumber said, looking at the sink.

He asked me if we had used Drano, Liquid Plumber or any of the other stuff to try to get the sink unclogged.

"No," I replied. "My parents were afraid that stuff would ruin the pipes."

"Good thinking," he said to me. "Okay, let me take a look. Oh, and by the way, my name is Tony."

"I'm Chris," I said and we shook hands.

His palm felt moist as it held my hand tightly as we shook. Then, he stepped close to the sink and put his toolbox down on the floor, his back to me. His ass cheeks were two perfectly rounded melon-shaped globes in his work pants. He ran the water and sure enough it did not go down the drain.

"The problem is probably in the pipe," he said. "No doubt there's something jammed in there."

He squatted down and opened the cabinet under the sink where the pipe was. The way he was squatting caused the back of his work pants to press snugly against his exquisite rear end. My heart pounded harder and my knees felt weaker. I was able to see the waistband of his white underpants.

"Okay, I have to remove this pipe," he said, looking up at me. "But first do you think you can help me take all these pots and pans out from under here?"

"Sure," I replied.

He began handing me the pots and pans that my parents kept stored under the sink. I placed them all on the nearby dining room table. The kitchen in our house is not air conditioned so by the time we were done taking all the pots and pans out from under the sink we were both pretty sweaty.

"Okay, now I'll just turn off the main water valve under there and then I'll unscrew that pipe," Tony said and shucked off his black tee shirt. "Ah, now that's better."

Under his black tee shirt he was wearing a white tight fitting tank top. His arms, shoulders, and chest were <u>extremely</u> muscular. His nipples were pressing meanly against the thin cotton material of the tank top. His chest was hairy. He wiped his forehead with the black tee shirt and then his sweaty armpits.

"Man, it's hot!" he said with a smile and tossed the tee shirt to me.

I caught it with two hands and held it tightly. My hands were shaking and sweating.

"Yeah, I hate the summer heat," I said slowly as he raised his big arms above his head and stretched.

His armpits were extremely hairy and the way he stretched caused his tank top to move away from the sides of his nipples, exposing them. They were big, (the size of silver dollars) pink and extremely pointed in the surrounding dark hair all over his chest. My breath came slowly and I could feel my dick getting hard in my shorts. He lowered his arms, squatted by the sink, and opened his toolbox. I stood there transfixed as he reached under the sink and turned off the main water valve.

"There, now I'm ready," he said to me.

He took a big wrench out of his toolbox and slid his upper body under the sink. While he was busy unscrewing the pipe I raised his tee shirt slowly toward my face. I heard him grunting as he worked his long legs and booted feet visible from under the sink. I pressed one of the armpit sections of his moist tee shirt to my nose and mouth and inhaled deeply. It smelled <u>very</u> musty, pungent, and raw with his body odor. The man definitely did not use deodorant. I closed my eyes and again inhaled the scent of his tee shirt. When I opened my eyes he was looking at me, smiling, watching me sniff his rancid tee shirt. My eyes opened wide in panic and I dropped his tee shirt to the floor. He simply squatted there, smiling at me. God, that smile.

"You like the way my tee shirt smells from my sweaty armpits eh Chris?" he asked me lustfully.

"I-uh, I…" I stammered nervously.

He stood straight up, bent over to pick up his tee shirt, and stepped close to me.

"It's okay guy," he said and handed the tee shirt back to me. "Go ahead."

Staring into his eyes I again brought the armpit section of his tee shirt to my nose and mouth. I inhaled deeply, and reached out. I hooked my thumb and first finger around one of the straps of his white tank top.

"Tony," I whispered breathlessly and gave his sleeve a tug, looking at the big nipple under it.

I let go of his tank top and took another hearty sniff of his tee shirt.

"Yeah, you like that all right," Tony said to me and raised his arms above his head. "And I bet you'd like the real thing even more. I bet you'd just love to eat these stinky pits of mine."

He took a sniff of one of his rancid pits and I dropped his tee shirt to the floor.

"Oh yeah," I said just above a whisper.

"Go for it guy," Tony said, looking at me intently.

I placed my hands on his sides and moved my face close to his left armpit. I inhaled once, twice, three times. The odor was overpowering, rancid, and awesome at the same time. Tony held his arms up, his fingers of both hands entwined behind his head. I pressed my lips against his hairy armpit, held them there, and inhaled with my nose again. Heaven, to say it plainly. Tony's big bushy armpits smelled funky from his sweat. They were deliciously moist. I stuck out my tongue and licked his armpit.

"Ohhh yeah," Tony said breathlessly. "Feels so good."

I licked his hairy pit all over and all around. He closed his eyes and tilted his head back, a look of ecstasy on his beautiful face, his armpits stretched out for me.

"Ohhhh yeah, my pits sweat so much in this blasted heat," Tony moaned. "Lick 'em clean for me Chris, oh yeah, lick my smelly pits."

I wrapped my arms around Tony's waist and held him tight as I tongue bathed his left armpit. My dick was hard, thick, and pounding with a life of it's own in my shorts. After a while Tony's armpit hair was soaked with my saliva. I dribbled into his pit and quickly sucked up my juices. When his left armpit was clean and fresh smelled I moved my head over to his right one.

"Oh yeah Chris, lick that one for me too," Tony whispered. "Clean it up good, yeah, lick my pits."

As I went to work sniffing Tony's right armpit I ran my hands up and down his muscular back, hugging him to me, holding him tight. His back was rippled with muscles. God almighty, he felt and smelled so fucking good. I was in utter ecstasy as I stuck out my tongue and buried it in his thick armpit hair. I slid the tip of my tongue through his armpit hair and then all around the outer edges of it. My hands moved downward and found his tight melon-shaped butt cheeks. I squeezed them hard. Tony moaned gently and in that manly passion with his head still tilted back and his eyes closed.

"You taste so good," I said and kissed his armpit hard before slurping a good mess of his sweat out of it.

When I was done cleaning his right armpit I held him tighter and tighter and moved my head back to his left armpit. I kissed it all over again and again and again. Finally, Tony opened his eyes, looked down at me, and lowered his arms. He smiled as I ran my hands over his chest and kissed it.

"You really are some armpit licker," he said. "My pits never get such good treatment.

We looked at each other, smiled, and kissed on the lips. As our tongues explored each other's mouths I ran my hands over the back of Tony's neck, stroking his silky black hair. God, I wanted to touch him everywhere. As I kissed him and kissed him I rolled his tank top up till his nipples were visible. I squeezed them gently ands we stopped kissing.

"Damn, looks like you're after those nips of mine now, eh Chris?" Tony asked me. "I'll never get to fix that sink at this rate."

Tony leaned up against the wall, once again clasped his hands up behind his head, and moaned in ecstasy as I sucked his nipples alternately and rubbed his exposed armpits with the palms of my hands.

"Oh yeahhh, work on me Chris," Tony moaned in total ecstasy. "Suck my big fleshy nips, oh yeah, suck 'em."

Tony's armpits were still moist with my saliva and as I sucked his nipples he started sweating all over again. It was obvious to me that his armpits would need some attention again, attention that I did not mind giving them. The bulge in Tony's work pants looked like it was ready to burst through his underwear and pants. When I stopped sucking Tony's nipples they were erect and hard to the touch. His armpits were newly wet with sweat. He didn't lower his arms this time. He knew or expected that I would gladly service his armpits again. I leaned in close to Tony's left armpit, kissed it a few times, and then went to work on it with my tongue.

"Oh yeah, clean my pits again Chris," Tony moaned in manly passion. "They sweat so much…"

As I licked, sucked, slurped, and kissed Tony's armpits all over again I squeezed his erect nipples at the same time. They felt super hard to the touch.

"Ohhhhrrr God, I'm so horny Chris," Tony said through clenched teeth, a look of sheer ecstasy all over his face. "You're making me want to cum like crazy."

I moved my hands down to the zipper on Tony's work pants and pulled it down, licking his armpits feverishly as I did so.

"Ohhh yes," he moaned in passion.

I reached into the fly opening of Tony's pants, past his briefs, and pulled out his dick. It was hard as rock, long, fat, and pulsing with heat and energy. Pre cum oozed out of his dick slit. I closed my hand around his dick and stroked it slowly as I continued licking his armpits.

"Ohhhhh shit, yeahhhh Chris, yeah," Tony whispered breathlessly. "Make me cum, oh yeah, make me shoot my load."

I purposely stroked him slowly, wanting him to enjoy how I was licking his armpits. God knew I was enjoying licking the fuck out of them. Tony was sweating more and more at this point.

"Oh gads, I'm getting close now Chris," Tony panted. "I'm going shoot a monster sized load, oh yeah."

Tony shot his load a few minutes later, cumming in my hand. I managed to catch as much of it as possible in my hands.

"Ohhhhh yeahhhh! Yeah! Fuckin' A!" Tony roared as I stroked him and stroked him, his cum bubbling in thick ropes from his slit.

He writhed in ecstasy against the wall with his arms still up behind his head.

"Ohhhhh yeah Chris, yeahhhh, milking me like crazy, making me shoot my load, making me fucking cum!" Tony panted breathlessly.

When he was done I smeared his cum all over his bushy armpits, rubbing it in with my hands and the tips of my fingers. I wasn't able to leave his pits alone.

"You're a sleazy guy Chris," Tony said with a smile as I began licking his cum off his hairy armpits.

He stood there looking so fucking hot. His tank top was still rolled up above his nipples, his arms were still crossed behind his head, and his dick was still hanging out of the fly opening of his work pants, semi hard. I licked his armpits, sucked on them, kissed them, and licked them some more. I couldn't get enough of them. In between licking Tony's pits I stole sucks on his nipples, holding him tightly around his waist.

"Can't get enough of your sweaty pits and tits," I whispered.

A few minutes later Tony's dick was hard again and pulsing between his legs. I slid to my knees and gobbled the giant tube steak into my mouth.

"Ohhhhh, Ohhhhhrrr gads, yeahhhh!" Tony roared, looking down at me in ecstasy. "Suck my meat Chris, yeahhh…"

He moved his arms down to his sides and caressed the back of my neck as I sucked his big dick. It tasted as good as his armpits, which I intended to get back to as soon as I had made the hot plumber shoot a second load. I sucked Tony's dick like crazy, poking my tongue into his piss slit, dribbling all over it, and sucking my saliva up off it. He made his hands into fists and swiveled his body seductively in front of me, dancing with his dick in my mouth as I sucked him harder and harder. He was sweating in and stinking in ecstasy all over again. There was no doubt in my mind that his armpits would need to be cleaned up again.

"Ohhhhrrr God, going to make me shoot another load," Tony roared. "Never came twice so soon. Ohhh man, you're fucking driving me crazy Chris!"

I sucked the guy till I thought he was going to topple over. He slammed his muscular body against the wall, squeezed his nipples hard, and shot his second load, right into my mouth. As he came I continued sucking him, sending him into a sexual and heated frenzy.

"Ohhhhh fuck, yeahhhh!" Tony cried out loudly.

When he was done this time I let his big dick slip out of my mouth. (Reluctantly I might add.) I stood up and we put our arms around each other. The big guy rested his head on my shoulder and I held him as tightly as possible, not wanting to let go of him, ever. I kissed his neck and nipped at his earlobes, sucking on them. Tony kissed my neck and hugged me tight, breathing heavily. A few moments later I was sitting on a chair with Tony kneeling in front of me. He slowly unlaced my sneakers and slid them off my feet. He raised one of my sneaker scented feet to his face and sniffed it.

"Mmmmm…" he crooned and ran his tongue along the side of my bare foot.

As Tony licked my foot my dick grew hard in my shorts. I watched in awe as the gorgeous plumber held my foot lovingly in his hands and serviced it with his tongue.

"Ohhhh Tony, yeahhh…" I moaned.

He sucked my toes like they were dicks, swirling his tongue around each one while he had it in his mouth. I was in ecstasy now. I never knew how good it could feel to have someone lick my smelly feet and suck my toes. When Tony was done with both my feet he rested his head in my lap. I stroked his beautiful hair and caressed the back of his neck. Then, he unzipped my shorts and I fed him my hard dick. He slurped it in his mouth and sucked it for all he was worth.

"Ohhhh yeah, yeahhh," I crooned happily.

When I shot my load Tony caught my cum in his hands. Kneeling in front of me he smeared my cum into his armpits.

"Ready to service my pits again Chris?" Tony asked me eagerly.

"You don't need to ask," I responded just as eagerly.

That night when my parents came home from work they asked me if the plumber had come and if he fixed the sink. I told them that he had definitely come and that he needed to come again the next day to finish the job.

■

Shoeshine

Enhanced by: Christopher Trevor

It was supposed to have been a shoeshine, just an ordinary old fashioned shoeshine, that day when I had gone dashing out of my Wall Street office because I had gotten stuck working late…again… Just an ordinary old shoeshine, which turned into one of the kinkiest and most erotic experiences of my entire life…

The problem had appeared in the accounting department's computer system, of course just before quitting time and so, as often happens I knew that at 4:30 Id be putting the extra time in. I didn't really have any plans that evening but it was still frustrating to have to stay late, since I was heading to the L.A. office the next day, early, and I had been planning to get some errands done and then relax before my business trip. So much for that I told myself as I packed up my backup discs and after all the turmoil of the accounting department's computer problem had been rectified I made my way to the elevator. It was now 7:05 PM and the office was deserted, everyone no doubt already at home having dinner, as I stood around waiting, making mental notes of what to pack for tomorrow's business trip. (As I stood there waiting for the elevator I thought about some of those handsome young executive hunks in my office. I thought of those married studs at home now, having dinner with their sexy wives, sitting there at the table in their shorts, tee shirts and their dark dress socks still on them after having gotten out of what we Wall Street boys call the monkey suit. I know that a lot of those muscle execs leave their dress socks on at the end of the day, knowing that without even mentioning it how their wives are erotically attracted to the stink of their socks and feet after having been encased in their leather wingtips or cap toes all damned day.) The weather had begun to get hot already, though you wouldn't know it from our air-conditioned office, so I could probably stand to pack those filmy white shorts I had bought at Macy's and a couple of the hot looking tank tops for after hours play. God, I know how so many studs out there just love stripping a guy like me out of his business (monkey) suit and finding a stringy tank top under his shirt, rather than a traditional man's undershirt. Those stringy tank tops sure do show off the nipples and pecs in just the right way bud, let me tell you. And if I may say so myself I'm pretty stacked up in the nipples and pecs areas. I felt myself gearing up for those Hollywood bars and all those exhibitionist blond studs packed into their tight 501's with their muscular bodies and blue eyes...

Stepping into the elevator I was glad that I had maintained my gym discipline and I stretched long and hard, feeling my muscular arms against the smooth cotton of my tailored shirt and flexing my muscular ass in the curve of the gabardine. The job that I have can be beyond demanding at times but the money was worth it, especially when I could combine some work down south with a little pleasure. I adjusted my crotch, feeling my balls churn and my cock get hard just thinking about cruising those southern California beach boys, remembering past trips, the sweat, the longing, the tight feel of a new muscle boy body in the cool, crisp hotel room. As the elevator opened the warm moist air of the lobby covered my face like a soothing insistent hand, sliding over my chin and eyelids, highlighting the moist patches of sweat under my arms and around my now hard nipples. Hearing the click, clack of my heels on the marble of the dimly lit lobby I realized at that moment that I had not managed to get my shoes shined for tomorrow's trip. I had intended to do it at lunch but because I had been so stressed out from all the work I had totally forgotten about it. Then, to my surprise the light in the shoeshine kiosk in the lobby of my office building was still, oddly, lit. Usually my buddy Ben closed up at 5:00 sharp, but I heard him rattling about in the small enclosure, so I thought that he was probably just getting ready to go, also thinking that he must have had a rush of customers today to be there so late in the evening. Poking my head around the corner into the smallish space built into the end of the unused hallway to the stairs I said, "Hey Ben, got time for one more? I've got a business trip tomorrow and I have to look my best."

Perhaps it was my slight fatigue and relaxation, perhaps it was the new summer air and the dark abandoned feel of the building, perhaps it was my own unconscious fantasy, but when Ben looked at me I realized that his smile and quiet assent of, "Sure Mr. Young, I'll do you up fine," had a delightful effect on me. Perhaps it was my imagination, but did the shoeshine guy look me over up and down in a lustful way, his eyes seeming to be riveted on my shoes for more than a few seconds as he looked down at my feet? Not that I had never noticed him at all before. He was a young, slim and energetic black man, maybe around 20 years old, with a body no clothes could really conceal very well. He was extremely handsome actually, a tiny waist built up into a tense and chiseled chest and forearms that he displayed in tight white tee shirts worn thin in places, sloping down into equally tight jeans that pulled on his high round ass and big thighs, an ass and thighs too big for the cut of his jeans so that the bulge of his crotch stood out, shifting as he stood facing me, his black gloved hands holding two big gleaming wooden-mounted brushes. He had been doing my shoes for as long as I had worked there, in the same space, hardly bigger than a slightly expanded closet furnished with two straight back chairs mounted high on a platform and footrests of worked metal. Ben had told me a while back that shining shoes helped to pay for his college education. He attended classes' part time. Usually, despite that beautiful body I thought no more of him than I imagined he of me, since during the day he usually had a couple of buddies around and they shot the shit about horses, girls and their classes in college. Tonight, however, the mood seemed different, the air was heavier, and as our eyes met and he stole glances down at my feet he let that sly smile creep out of the side of his mouth.

"Sure, we'll do you up just fine," Ben said, sounding lustful again as he spoke.

He pointed the brush at one of the chairs and tugged at his crotch. An unconscious gesture?

"Got to look nice huh?" the shoeshine guy asked me with that lusty grin. "Don't want you traveling with your shoes all a mess, do we Mr. Young?"

Without replying to what he had just asked me I mounted the two steps to the platform where I sat down, high up, my crotch at Ben's eye level. Watching me out of the corner of his eye he put his brushes down and slid his gloves off. The way that the footrests were mounted required that I scoot my hips forward some, my butt resting almost on the edge of the chair while I leaned back, spreading my legs high apart. This hiked my suit pants up, displaying the black Italian slip-ons I was wearing and the nylon navy blue calf length ribbed socks I had been given once for Christmas. Ben stood between my legs and looked up into my eyes, his eyes telling a story all their own as he took his time setting down his buffing brushes and with gentle movements rolled my cuffs up a couple of times, really displaying my navy blue socks now. His fingers grazed my nylon socks as he began to chat in his lazy and sexy way.

"Working late Mr. Young?" he asked me as he rubbed the outside edge of my shoes with his fingers, caressing the leather and the top of my foot as well.

He even went so far as to pull my socks up to my calves for me, seeing as they had drooped down slightly during the day, which I suppose is true for most guy's socks. Then, after pulling my socks up he rolled my cuffs up a few more times. Now my nylon navy blue socks were REALLY on display let me tell you.

"Always liked your shoes and socks Mr. Young, good leather your shoes are made of," he went on, sounding sexier yet as he spoke, squeezing my socked calf a couple of times. "They take a great shine from me when I work on 'em for you. And your socks too…always so silky looking and stylish…"

He continued to rub the shoes then from heel to toe and the leather was so supple that it felt more like a foot massage was happening as his fingers ran down my insteps to my toes and back up the top of my foot to the ankle. He didn't take his eyes from me and I saw a small rivulet of perspiration make its way down his chest as he stood between my legs and began to rub the polish on my shoes with a small round brush. I was riveted to this sight, feeling vulnerable somehow and hot and all worked up as he bent over and worked on my feet, his brown muscles shifting and moving. A few times as he rubbed the polish onto my shoes he would snap the elastic in my socks against my calf, grinning as he did so, saying things like, "Great socks too, nice nylon silky feel to 'em." My cock was getting hard, my armpits were wet and oh God, my mind raced. Could he actually know what I wanted? Could he know how all this was turning me on? Did he think that I would actually go through with this, right here in his small enclosed space in the lobby of the building where I worked? My expression must have tipped him off, for I felt somehow hypnotized by his gentle persistent rubbing and the long slow sexy drawl of his conversation. He then rested his hand on my foot for a moment and with a deft flick of the wrist shut the sliding door behind him, enclosing us in the kiosk. I stifled a gulp by pursing my lips tightly together.

"You know Ben, this feels very good," I managed to tell him, my lips dry and hot after I managed to un-purse them.

"Sure it does Mr. Young," the handsome black guy said to me with a grin, displaying his pearly whites. "You're a man who likes nice things; likes to feel good don't you? Like these pretty nylon silky socks that go way up to your calves."

He then slid a finger up to my calf along the side of one of my socks and with a shock I suddenly felt a tremor run through my entire muscular body, God, from the tips of my toes to the crown of my head and back. This time I could not purse my lips in time, this time I let out an involuntarily moan.

"I think you're a little ticklish Mr. Young, hmm?" he asked me and did it again, this time using his nail, a hard little edge up both my socked calves this time from the soft tender spot right behind my ankle.

I almost lifted myself up right out of the chair, stifling my laughter, but Ben grabbed my feet and held them down.

"Woooey! Mr. Young, you've been working just way too hard, I can see that now, just by how jumpy you are," Ben went on laughingly. "You're all stressed out, as you Wall Street boys always say. I don't know if you should be wearing these little slipper like shoes where you can feel everything I touch, seeing as you're all tense and…"

"And stressed out, yeah, that's the expression Ben, the one we Wall Street boys use," I said, repeating what he'd said just moments before.

He circled the stiff brush over my toes, which I started to flex and wiggle in my socks while at the same time trying to get away from the touch of his damned brushes, but also at the same time finding myself craving it. I wanted it, I didn't want it, and I found myself breathing hard all of a sudden, squirming in the seat, listening to Ben go on about my shoes and socks in his smooth deep sexy voice.

"And I'm not even touching your feet Mr. Young, just shining your shoes," he said. "Tell you what, why don't you just sit there and let me work on you? I'll get you good and ready for tomorrow. Close your eyes Mr. Young let me do my work. Know what I'm saying Sir?"

He moved the bristles close to the edge of the tongue of the shoe, leaning against the front of my legs with his one arm, holding me still as I bucked reflexively, relentlessly swiping the tops of my feet with big strokes, back and forth and back and forth and back and forth. My toes were curled up tight and hard in a vain attempt to protect myself...

"Oh Ben, come on man, *I can't stand it...*" I mumbled sounding very sexy.

He laughed throaty and full.

"You're standing it just fine Mr. Young," the shoeshine stud said to me. "Why, you even like it I think."

Then, his fingers started exploring the soft flesh around my ankle bones and every time I twisted my feet from side to side I was met with a probe, a squeeze or some light little touch that made me start to chuckle.

"See? I told you. You like it Mr. Young," Ben teased me. "You are a man who needs some good laughs after a hard day of work, to relieve all that stress you Wall Street boys endure all day."

He increased the speed of the tickling, alternating sides then suddenly switching rhythms, keeping me kind of off guard, and I was afraid I was going to end up kicking him, all the muscles in both my legs flexing and squeezing right up to my crotch and back again. (But Ben would remedy the situation of my almost kicking him very soon bud.) I started laughing really hard, my sweaty palms slipping against the arms of the chair as I slid lower and lower into Ben's clutches.

"Give it up to me baby, give it to me Mr. Young," Ben said in a sing-song type of voice as he sprayed some clear looking stuff on my shoes, making sure to keep his face away from the stuff, then raising the spray can and quickly spraying some of the sickly scented stuff in my nose and mouth.

I didn't know what the stuff was except that he sprayed more of it on my shoes and I felt now like I was floating on the chair as the guy worked on getting my shoes polished...

The heat building up in the compartment and the thick smells of his sweat, the scent of whatever he sprayed at me and the scent of the polish compelled me to follow his order. I leaned my head back and closed my eyes as he backed off and then just continued rubbing the brushes against my shoes. I was breathing hard, in a stupor of sorts when he came around from behind me, slipped off my suit jacket and ran his slim hand down my shoulders and arms to the fingertips, down my thighs in my gabardine suit pants, over my knees and then back to home base at my socked ankles and shoed feet where he dipped the brush into the polish another time, continuing to apply it to my shoes. The waxy aroma mixed with our own sexual scent. My feet were more than tingling right through the leather of my shoes at that point and God; I felt a big wet patch growing in my shorts under my suit pants. When I opened my mouth to speak I received another nose and mouthful of the spray from Ben's can for my trouble. I gurgled and leaned my head back involuntarily…

"Man, oh man, got me a real handsome executive here," Ben crooned delightedly as I sat there in a stupor, my boner more than evident now in my suit pants. "Oh yes, I know what you executive type men like, how uncomfortable it can be sitting still when you feel so damned good at the same time…"

I then felt a flurry of deft movements around my ankles, not really tickling this time, though by now just breathing on my feet would have driven me crazy, and when I squirmed to protect myself I found that Ben had expertly and quickly tied my navy blue socked ankles to the footrests with a couple of belts. He stared me straight in the eyes, a devious smile playing across his moist and sexy lips, running his hand now up and down my socks. Then, he reached around behind me and took a pair of Velcro straps off the wall where they usually held a pair of big shoe brushes, and with similar speed looped these around my wrists to lash them down to the armrests of the chair. I couldn't resist, not with those seductive eyes keeping me in my place, and not to mention whatever he had sprayed in my nose and mouth to make me so helplessly docile and the smell and feel of him all over me, and with all my muscles straining and quivering. I wanted more; I wanted him to drive me insane. That's how it happened man, that's how I gave myself over to this masterful young man and his beautiful hands. Turned on beyond belief I let myself be vulnerable, let him render me unable to move, while I watched him through my half-closed eyelids, watched him savor me with his dark eyes lustfully from below.

"You are such a handsome executive guy, so strong and smooth Mr. Young," Ben prattled on, driving me nuts as he caressed my socked calves.

His blunt fingers found their way to my shirt and he purposely ran his fingers across my ribs. Unable to move I found that all I could do was cry out and laugh, arching my muscular back which just made him laugh and poke a little harder.

"Ha, ha, ha, ha, ha, ha, ha!" was the sound coming from me and filling the small enclosed space we were in.

"Can't even take your shirt off can I without you wiggling around like crazy?" he punctuated his taunting with more pokes. "Can I?"

"N-no!" I gasped and wiggled uncontrollably.

Fuck, it was useless.

"No! No!" I squealed again.

Every poke pumped a cry out of me, a moan, a chuckle, a guffaw…

"Can I?" Ben asked and poked my ribs again.

"No!" I replied. "Ha, ha, ha, ha, ha, ha!"

The chair squealed along with me as I thrashed around uselessly.

"No! No! Ha, ha, ha, ha!" I chortled.

My damp chest was now exposed and he pulled my shirt and askew necktie up and over the chair, stretching it tight with my arms still in the sleeves in such a way as to batten my arms down firmly, as if in a straitjacket.

"Look at you tempting me with those big man pecs and big womanly tits of yours," Ben said, hanging his long tongue out of his mouth and taking little licks at each of my very erect nipples while continuing to stare straight into my eyes.

I was so electrified by the tickling and bondage I realized then that I had my back permanently arched my swollen nipples were high and erect like never before. Ben took full advantage of the situation by licking and nursing like crazy at what he called my womanly tits.

"N-not there, please Ben," I mumbled.

Even without all this foreplay my nipples were always incredibly sensitive, and trying madly to protect them by hunching my shoulders I bucked from side to side as I heard Ben begin to laugh.

"They're blooming bigger and bigger Mr. Young," the shoeshine stud guy said, nipping at my erect nubs with his front teeth.

He grazed his soft lips across the tops of them and I began to whine loud and high, like a siren of sorts, each of my cries ending in convulsive laughter.

"Yes Sir, they are blooming like little flower buds," he said and nipped them some more.

"Oh God," I gasped when I could. "Oh God, Ben please, ha, ha, ha, ha, ha!"

But it seemed that any time I could form a word Ben took that as a cue to tickle my nipples some more, this time switching between nearly intangible caresses with his lips and plucks with all five of his fingertips, each time causing me to shriek incoherently.

"Now that's what I want to hear Mr. Young," Ben said seductively. "Guys like you; you important Wall Street boys, you all talk way too much. Talking too much on the phone, talking too much in your board meetings, you Wall Street suit boys never take the time to laugh a while..."

I went to say something, to beg, to scream, flailing madly against the restraints, but he never let me catch my breath, playing his fingers down my side until my head started to swim from lack of air and my chest felt like it was going to burst.

"Ha, ha, ha, ha, ha!" I laughed and laughed, my voice carrying out to the building lobby.

Luckily no one was out there to hear my mad peals of laughter...

The whole world had turned into this small hot cubicle and the touch of Ben's cruel fingers. Again he sprayed whatever was in that spray can in my face, getting it right where he wanted it, in my nose and mouth...

"Huhhhhhhhhh..." I breathed deeply and the world spun and spun some more.

I must have passed out that time for more than a few moments because I came to with the comforting feeling of Ben stroking my navel with the back of his hand, my belly slick with what I could smell was the mineral oil he used to put a final sheen on the shoes he shined.

"Wh-what is that stuff you sprayed in my face man?" I asked him. "My God man, I was out cold..."

"See, you needed a little rest didn't you?" he asked me snidely. "Working way too hard, just like I said."

Unbelievably he had unbuckled my belt and opened up my suit pants and the crotch was flipped wide open. My briefs were totally visible. Ben moved the back of his hand down some and began to rub along the shaft of my cock, after he'd gotten it freed from my underpants, not all that gently I might add...

"Like I said, way too hard Mr. Young," he said with that grin of his and exhausted as I was I felt my hips buck up to meet his touch.

My cock was totally erect and sticking out of my suit pants now, what a sight that was bud! The shoeshine guy was playing me like a doll, like a goddamned toy, like I was a helpless play thing. He saw that though and laughed at me.

"You're all hard and oozing pre seed Mr. Young," he said, grasping my manhood in his fist. "Sure sign that you like this."

I couldn't answer, not with my cock in his hand, which put him off a bit it seemed because he took the edge of his thumbnail and dragged it up the shaft of my big pulsing manhood… That pumped me up good and straight let me tell you and I gave out a loud whoop sound.

"Oh no, not again man," I blubbered.

"Say you like it, tell me you like this," Ben commanded.

He grabbed little pinches of flesh around my navel with one hand and scraped my cock-head with the other, forcing it out of me, tickling me till I did what he wanted.

"I do Ben, I do, oh God, *I do*," I gurgled in between laughter.

"Want what?" he asked me snidely.

Every touch sent jolts straight into my pelvis, my asshole clenched, sweat pouring from my most private of crevices, my hips fucking the air while I howled with laughter.

"You! You man, I want you! Ha, ha, ha, ha!" I chortled crazily. "Oh stop it, please stop it!"

"Who?" he asked me and kept up the dissonant pinching and stroking, my knees forced wide with his chest between them, all of him on top of me, holding me down and tormenting me. "What?"

"You, tickling me, I want it, ohhhhhh my God, I want it man!" I guffawed. "Ha, ha, ha, ha!"

"Say don't stop," Ben commanded.

"D-don't stop! Ben, don't stop, don't stop, ha, ha, ha, ha!" I laughed and laughed.

I was drooling by now, each word coming out with a boom of hilarity and ending in a long painful moan. Ben was calm though and amused at the same time.

"Okay then, how about my specialty now?" he asked me, as if I had a choice in the matter.

He proceeded to pull my suit pants down and then pulled my briefs down next, taking his time by tucking the waistband of them under my churning and sweaty balls, which made my huge pre cumming and wet cock stand up straighter than straight in front of his hungry face.

"Now Mr. Young, I got some toys here, tools of the trade you know," he chuckled as he opened a drawer of brushes with long luxurious bristles, some like paint brushes with long stiff handles, others like shoe-shining brushes only thin and cushioned.

As I looked at his drawer filled with what he called his tools of the trade I also took in the sight of myself with my suit pants hiked down around my knees, my under shorts tucked under my big balls, lashed to a shoeshine chair. God almighty, if my office buddies could see me now I thought. Ben took one of the long handled paint brushes and dipped it into a can of clear shoe wax, working the paste soft and then with long, exquisite motions began to stroke my free standing cock, using the bristles to get under the head, poking my piss slit and using his other hand to milk the shaft until more and more pre cum dripped down. Every part of me was wrenching with spasms by now, he had gotten me so sensitized and excited, but I had never had someone take a brush to my slit. What a sensation man! The effect of it made me want to dig my ass deep into the chair, as if I could retract my cock from the strokes, but of course all of it was in vain. The way Ben had me tied to the chair at the wrists and ankles I was totally in his power man. I couldn't move, I didn't want to, and at a certain point after the brush got good and slimy from the oil, the sweat and my pre cum the tip of it started reaching deep inside my now gaping cock head. Good God almighty bud, it was like a switch had been turned on in my hips and with a lurch my whole body went stiff as a board, my cock thrust out for him, as if I had no other use in the world except to give the shoeshine guy all of the most tender parts of me to titillate and torture erotically. He sprayed some more of whatever was in that spray can in my nose and mouth and I floated off as he tortured my cock and balls with that damned brush.

"That's right, now you're learning Mr. Young," Ben said meanly and sprayed still more of the stuff in my face just for fun it seemed. "Got to teach you what you're good for handsome man."

My head lolled back and forth from the effects of what he had sprayed at me… It smelled sickly and yet it got my blood flowing even as I swooned in a stupor of sorts…

"Don't pull back Mr. Young, ask for it," the shoeshine guy said to me. "Ask for it. You love it."

My teeth were clenched and my eyes rolled up into my head, the effects of the contents of the spray can no doubt. He kept at my hot wet cock with his collection of brushes, going down the line systematically, jacking me off man, jacking me off leisurely as he retired one brush and dipped the bristles of another in the oil or the clear paste. A few times in between all this he sprayed the spray can contents in my face, keeping me good and docile and under his control…

"Some of these are harder than others Mr. Young," Ben explained with cool but wicked glee as he waxed up another brush, this one with softer bristles, and ran it in short hard strokes right over the blood engorged crown of my harder than hard cock.

God, could something hurt and feel so good at the same time?

"Man oh man, you are hard as a rock my handsome executive," Ben said delightedly. "I bet I could take needles to this head of yours. Just look at that Mr. Young, just look at yourself."

His voice was coming from far away it seemed, but when he reached up and forced my head down to look I knew that he was right there.

"Look at how hard you are Mr. Young," he repeated. "You're loving this ain't you? All slimy and oozing your pre seed like crazy too."

At that point he started to tap my corona with the brush, batting it from side to side, catching the ridge of my cock and making me squeal.

"Too much! *That's too much man!"* I began to cry and laugh all at the same time. "Oh God, nooooooooo!"

Gasping, I felt him stop, massaging the whole length of my cock now with his soft hands, comforting me, letting me breathe, letting whatever the shit in the spray can was wear off finally.

"Too much huh Mr. Young?" he asked me snidely. "So maybe you'll like this some then."

He eagerly removed a fleecy chamois cloth wet with oil from the back of the drawer. Holding it in both hands he looped it over the slippery head of my cock and began to draw it with hard quick pressure toward him, hitting the shaft as if buffing it, the edge of the cloth occasionally hitting beneath the ridge of my crown and creating a kind of wild, painful friction that both hurt and made me even hungrier to cum. My cock bounced up and down and my thighs twitched. It was intolerable it made me ache to put my wet cock somewhere, in Ben's velvet mouth, up his hard ass, somewhere, thrusting into the air.

"Oh ho! Oh Ho! Ho, ho, ho, ho, ho, ho, ho, ho!" I was screaming in laughter as he ran the cloth over my cock like a saw, but of course he still had more tricks up his sleeve. And to get more for his money he stuck out his index fingers and ended every stroke with a good solid poke in my sides, making me almost want to jump out of my skin between the buffing and tickling. He kept it up in a quick rhythm until I was really doing nothing but just yelling and laughing at the top of my lungs, at which point he took the cloth, wrapped it tight around my cock and let me collapse into the chair. Here he stopped for a while, and while I lay there in the chair trying to come to my senses, panting, waiting for more, my chest running with sweat, I had to cum, I just had too, I recall thinking that somehow I wanted to touch my cock and bring myself off. But being tied to the chair at my wrists I couldn't, and in this state of aching and intense desire Ben just let me sit there, half naked, totally aroused, very teased, overly sensitized and bound... He sprayed more of that sickly scented stuff in my face and it was more than a few minutes later when I opened my eyes...

"G-good God," I said softly as I came around.

"You like that Mr. Young?" Ben asked me. "You like my brushes?"

I licked my lips and gazed at him wordlessly, gazed at him in total disbelief actually, and nodding my head, entranced and greedy for the pleasure he gave me. Here, seeing my need he decided to play with me some more, cruelly leaving me stranded even longer at the edge of orgasm.

"How about this Mr. Young?" he asked me, sounding sexy and sultry at the same time. "You'll like this."

He stripped off his wet tee shirt and flexed his muscles for me, cupping his brown nipples and pulling on the tips of his glossy chocolate chips, running his hands over the ripples in his belly and down into his jeans which had now tented out with an enormous, hidden erection.

"Or maybe you like this more?" he asked and turned around and wiggled his solid butt cheeks out of the confines of his jeans, letting the waistband push his ass up hard and high as he stroked it for me, looking over his shoulder at me, gauging my expression.

My cock pounded harder and harder...

"Ben, please man, *please,* let me cum, God, I'm going to pass out, please man, this is all so good," I said, barely able to speak at that point, my lungs and chest so sore from the laughter, my cock pulsing from all he'd done to it with his brushes and oils, my head spinning from whatever he had sprayed in my nose and mouth.

Naked before me, seeming bigger as he pushed apart my thighs he teased me some more, blowing on the head of my cock, making it twitch and strain some more. Pre cum oozed steadily out of the hole and down into the pouch of underwear beneath my churning balls.

"Say please again Mr. Young and then I'll finish you off," Ben teased me mercilessly. "Say Please Ben baby, do me now."

My body writhed with the orgasmic tension as I imagined those full moist lips of his on my cock, drinking my cum.

"I want to hear it again Mr. Young, say it again," Ben whispered so fucking lustfully that it was driving me beyond insane.

How could he revel in this so much, this muscle stud shoeshine guy? How the hell could he mind fuck me so thoroughly? I felt tears well up, God!

"Please Ben baby, please do me," I heard myself saying desperately. *"Please, Ben, please…"*

My cock was engorged to its limit, swaying and pushing up into the air. I was afraid that he might start in again with the tickling, jamming his fingers into my ribs, poking my thighs, or worse yet maybe my neck or my balls, all the places where I'm devilishly ticklish that he hadn't gotten to yet. Tied up the way he had me I was afraid of him at this point, afraid that he might never let me go, that I might be kept here all weekend in the deserted office building, tortured out of my mind and at the mercy of his fingertips and tools. I had heard the stories of executives being kidnapped for ransom and such, I would be the first executive kidnapped for the purposes of tickle torture I would think. Although there was some guy named Timmy Backman. If I heard it correctly he was an executive kidnapped for tickle torture…or something like that thereof…

Beneath my chair I felt Ben switch something on that gave the whole platform a gentle vibration.

"See here Mr. Young, I have a special little helper, just for you," Ben said menacingly.

From underneath the chair he pulled out a small instrument which resembled an electric drill, but in place of the pointed drill was a huge soft white brush with bristles nearly two inches long, and as it spun around the brush flared into a wide tantalizing circle. Ben's fingers gripped the base of my cock, firmly holding my testicles against the chair to keep me still, and licking his lips he lowered the rotating head of the brush straight onto my cock, enveloping the wet sticky head of my pulsating organ into the soft swirling bristles. The brush was exquisitely soft, lubricated with God knows what, and the insistent vibration and rotation made me uncontrollable. Ben held me in place with his hot tight body wedged between my bucking thighs.

"Fuck, fuck, *fuck, fuck,*" I repeated senselessly, idiotically, my eyes shut tight.

I gripped the arms of the chair that my wrists were tied to and my knuckles turned pale white as my cock was being tortured toward a gusher like I never knew before…

"Let it come Mr. Young, fill my brush, let me see my executive guy shoot his pent-up load," Ben teased me and swirled the spinning brush over and over and over the crown of my engorged cock, down around the shaft of it and back up again, all while he was holding tight to my family jewels.

Grunting like an animal, my body one huge ticklish spasm I thought I might just tear the chair off the platform as I shot straight into the unending swirl of the brush, it was a devilish thing that brush. Then, I was pumping my cum out with rhythmic, breathless moans so that it flew in large droplets and spurts everywhere, against Ben's sweat-soaked face, against my gabardine suit pants, against my shirt, and oh God, even against the wall. Fuck, fuck, and fuck, I shot that high man. And still, *still* the brush bore down on my fat purple knob and gave it no rest, and God with the wicked ends of his fingers Ben added a small tickling to my ball sac which was drawn tight as an egg against the base of my spewing and spewing manhood. It seemed to go on and on as that swirling brush engulfed my cock and my cock spurted its hearty mess. Ben let out a loud whoop of laughter.

"Big executive man, big white man with his beautiful clothes needs me to show him, make him take it," Ben murmured. "Isn't that right Mr. Young?"

I was spent, beyond spent at that moment, unable to move, every inch of me wary that I might be touched, prodded, or made to scream with laughter some more after he took the cum soaked brush away from my cock. The crown of my cock was tingling and numb like I can't even describe to you... I couldn't speak, I couldn't swallow, I couldn't even groan. All I could do was watch Ben and listen to the sweet soft drone of his baritone voice.

"That's the way I like to see 'em, nice and relaxed Mr. Young," Ben went on. "I'll do almost anything to see that, I like that so very much, I do."

And with one more look at me laying there in his chair, still in his clutches, my fat cock drooping, the last remnants of cum dripping from my slit, all my muscles still twitching from the infernal tickling he had given me he laughed again, long, loud and deep.

"Wh-what now man?" I managed to whimper as he held up that spinning brush.

"It's a lot of work I know Mr. Young, but I've found that this is the best way to shine those pretty shoes like the ones you're wearing," Ben said. "You'll see."

With that he lowered the spinning brush filled with my cum directly onto the leather, he flashing his huge white wicked smile.

"This'll shine 'em up real nice now Mr. Young," Ben chuckled and I watched in awe as my cum was spread onto my shoes. "Real nice now, you'll see…"

To be continued…

■

The Bodybuilder

"Ohhhhhhh yeah, *yeah*, fucking A, lick my sweaty trunks you two wussies!" I moaned in a real man's passion as I sat on the top tier in the steam room at the gym. "Yeah, *yeah*, oh yeah, feels so fucking good your tongues on my silky Speedos! Lick my goddamned furry nuts through that sweaty silk you wussies! Treat my balls right! I love that feel of silk being licked against my gonads FUCK YEAH!"

My name is Eddie Valdez, Big Eddie to my weight lifting buddies at the gym that I go to on a regular goddamned basis. I'm six feet tall; I have black short cut hair, a thick mustache, and dark real sinister looking eyes. My body is built like a fucking brick shithouse from the daily workouts that I punish myself through at the gym. I'm thirty five years old, but with the shape I'm in you'd take me for a few years younger bud let me tell you. My legs are like two tree trunks, my thighs are strong enough to break coconuts between, and my stomach is hard as a rock and flat as a washboard, totally fucking ripped man. My shoulders are as wide as a goddamned doorway, my biceps are the size of bowling balls, my arms are long and sinewy with curled muscles, and my hands are as big as hams, big and strong enough to punch holes through walls with. My chest is robust and huge enough to eat a three course meal off of. (Actually, my chest and other parts of me have been used to eat meals off of, more on that another time though.) Two of the biggest, plumpest nipples adorn my huge chest, all day suckers as those two wussies of mine sometimes call them. What I want to tell you about happened a few months ago. I had taken the two faggots that live with me to the gym for a good hard workout. (It was a fucked up real estate agency that had sent me over to where the two faggots lived when I was apartment hunting. I didn't give a fuck that they were faggots that much I'll tell you. They were simply looking for a third occupant for the apartment to help pay the high rent.) Anyway, after I had gotten them into working out with me I found that I really liked forcing them through a good hard three to four hour workout every other day or so. Sometimes I even push them to four and a half hours if I feel that they can take it. If they workout well I allow them to worship my body as a reward. It was no secret that they were constantly salivating over me when I would come home after my workouts and parade around the house in just my underpants or the silk Speedos that I love so much. I figured what the fucking fuck; I paid my share of the rent, so I could parade around any which way I wanted. It was my apartment too after all. After we had worked out I brought them down to the locker room, told them to meet me in the steam room and proceeded to strip myself out of my gym clothes down to the navy blue silk (Speedo) bikini I was wearing instead of underpants. I like wearing silk Speedo bikinis instead of regular underpants because they feel awesome against my huge beefy cock and juicy hairy balls, something about that silk rubbing against my most private region really sets me in motion buds. But more to the point I like wearing silk Speedo bikinis instead of regular underpants because they stink like hell when you sweat in them and after a hard grueling workout my Speedos truly stench to the high heavens with my crotch smell let me tell you. They stink a lot worse and better than regular underpants do and my two wussies love sucking and licking the sweat out of my bikini, waiting for me to let them get at my giant cock and balls which bulge like crazy in there. I found out one night how much those two faggots loved my Speedos when I had gotten up to go to the bathroom. I walked into the bathroom and found that those two had rummaged through my hamper filled with my dirty clothes. They each had one of my Speedos in hand and they were sniffing them like they were the best smelling things on God's green earth. They thought at first that I would be pissed off at them, but instead I made them a deal, that if they wanted to lick and sniff my goddamned Speedos I wanted it done while I was wearing the fucking smelly things. Its not that I get off on two faggots licking my private areas, just that women I've dated would never get into something like that, and fuck it all buds, it feels great to have two tongues pressing that silky Speedo material against your crotch let me tell you... If you're a bodybuilder who has never experienced what I'm telling you about here find yourself two wussies who enjoy licking Speedo encased sweaty crotches and put them to work for you. Never fucking mind that maybe you're straight as a fucking arrow, just enjoy the feeling of those tongues on your sweaty Speedo and go with the flow.

When I got to the steam room I found my two wussies sitting on the tier below the top one. We seemed to be the last of the few members at the gym that night. No one to give us a hard time. I climbed to the top tier and leaned back in all my muscular and sweaty glory, my feet on the bottom tier. My two wussies sat between my legs on the second tier, looking hungrily upwards at my sweaty Speedo bikini. I ordered them to get busy. They instantly leaned forward and began licking and slurping and kissing my bikini. I closed my eyes, letting the steam caress me as my two wussies licked and sucked crazily at my bikini. The sounds of them working over my crotch area reverberated in the steam room. My huge cock was hard in no time and pressing against the silk material. My two wussies glided their tongues over my big furry balls through the silk material, sucking on them at the same time.

"Ohhhhhhhhh yeah, feels so FUCKING good," I crooned and ran a hand through my sopping wet and sweaty hair.

I crossed my huge arms up behind my head, exposing my hairy, sweaty, smelly armpits.

"Oh yeah, that's right guys, wussies, treat my trunks right," I said mockingly. "Then maybe I'll let you have at my armpits also."

I took a whiff of one of my rancid pits and told them how bad it stank. They ran their hands over my muscular thighs, squeezing them as they continued lapping like two dogs at my bikini. I knew that they wanted to suck me the fuck off. I knew that they wanted to see me cum. Greedy little faggots that they are they even liked swallowing my sexy jazz. Sometimes I would let them suck and pump three cum shots out of me, fuck, that's how much they loved to watch me jazz. I shoot real big fucking loads and they love it, *they fucking love it man*, they love watching the expressions on my face as I spurt and spew like a volcano for them. Sometimes when I cum they each take turns slurping my cock in and out of their mouths, the horny wussies each trying to chow down on as much of my sperm as possible; it's a real heady feeling let me tell you to have two faggots taking turns with your cock in their mouths while sperming. Other times they just jack me off in my Speedos, watching the expressions on my face as my sexy mess fills my goddamned smelly bikini…and then, oh God then, I watch as they eat my cum out of the Speedo, while I'm still wearing it, what a sight that is let me tell you, real sleazy.

As my two wussie slaves were licking, sucking and kissing my bikini the door to the steam room opened. Two guys, both of them pretty muscular walked in, each of them wearing only a towel around their waists. So much for us being the last of the members at the gym that night I thought.

"Holy fucking shit," the first guy said. "What in the hell is going on here?"

"We're servicing our master's Speedo," my first wussie slave said to the two men, saying it as if it was the most natural thing on earth that they were doing with me and my Speedo. "Join in on the fun if you want. There's more than enough of Big Eddie to go around…"

Before I could reprimand my wussie slave for treating me like I was a buffet for all to eat the two men were both kneeling at my size eleven feet. They each helped themselves, they each took one of my huge feet in their hands, lifted them to their mouths, and began licking them.

"Ohhhhhhh fuck, ohhh yeah," I groaned in ecstasy, lowering my arms. "Fuck, *fuck*, now I have four of you feasting on me. Go ahead you guys, lick my goddamned smelly feet, and chow down on my toes, don't forget to suck my goddamned toes…"

My two wussie slaves went on licking the sweat out of my bikini, not missing a beat and the two men were enjoying themselves licking my feet and sucking passionately on my toes. First they both sucked one of my big toes each, that really sent chills and thrills through me let me tell you. Then they each slurped a few of my smaller toes into their mouths and sucked heartily at those, same deal buds, chills and thrills abounded through my muscular being. It was obvious that these two were faggot foot freaks. Damn, why couldn't I find women that would do these sleazy things for me? I squeezed my hard and erect nipples and moaned in a man's passion. Fuck, whenever I as much as touch my big nipples it sends a thrill through my erection that is totally unfuckingbelievable. It feels like a very thin tube being inserted into my cock hole as I squeeze my big fat nipples. The heat of the steam was washing over all of us and I was in sheer ecstasy man. I leaned my head back, closed my eyes, and enjoyed, *I fucking enjoyed and enjoyed and enjoyed…* But then, the two men stopped licking my feet and sat up on the top tier at my sides. While my two wussies went on and on licking at my Speedo the two men pushed my huge arms up behind my head and ran their fingers over my sweaty, bushy and moist armpits.

"Man, I wonder if his pits taste as raunchy as his feet," the second guy chuckled.

"Only one way to find out," the first guy replied eagerly. "Hey Muscle guy, keep those big arms up behind your head, we're about to sample and service these hot lookin' pits of yours!"

"Fuckin' don't have to tell me twice you two," I said breathlessly.

I'm not used to taking orders where being serviced is concerned, but in this instance when the guy told me to keep my arms up behind my head I didn't object, fuck, what they were doing to me felt too goddamned good to object. The two men began sucking, licking, and kissing my sweaty, smelly armpits, stealing squeezes on my nipples at the same time. I was in the throes of sheer and utter ecstasy at that point. My muscular well toned body was a mess of goose bumps and I was sweating more and more. They would never finish licking all the man sweat off me; we were in a goddamned steam room after all. When I felt my Speedo bikini being pulled down in front I quickly opened my eyes. One of my wussie slaves was going after my hard cock without my fucking permission.

"HEY!" I yelled at him. "I do not recall saying that you could have my cock yet!"

"S-sorry Master Eddie," the wussie said and let go of my bikini.

"Wow, you really have them trained well," one of the guys licking my armpits said.

My two wussie slaves licked the outline of my hard cock and balls through my bikini some more. The two guys licking my armpits moved down to my nipples and they each helped themselves to one of them.

"Ohhhhhhhhrrrr yeah, suck my nips you two," I groaned loudly and placed my big hands on the backs of their necks.

At that moment the steam room door opened again, another guy walked in, and he without a single word knelt at one of my feet and began liking and kissing it feverishly.

"Fuck, holy fucking fuck, what a night this is turning out to be," I grunted. "Fuckin' got five guys swarmin' the fuck all over me…"

Then, one of my wussie slaves pulled my bikini down in the front again. Before I could yell at him to stop my giant cock and juicy furry balls were exposed for all to see, totally on display. My huge bodybuilder sized cock was harder than a rock and my balls were chock filled with my sexy mess and hanging low, real fucking low. My wussies always loved the way my big balls hung so provocatively between my thighs.

"Fuck, fuck, who gave you permission to go after my damned cock?" I yelled.

"Fuck permission man," one of the guys sucking my nipples said, taking a look down at my enormous beefy cock. "Fucking milk that crank of his…"

One of my wussie slaves opened his mouth wide and wrapped his lips tight around the top of my throbbing cock. Without my goddamned permission he began sucking it, trying so hard to get all of it into his mouth. Sweating more and more now my pre cum dripped down the shaft of my thick veined cock. The guy who was licking my feet moved his head close to my crotch and along with my other wussie slave began chowing down on my big smelly hairy balls. They licked, sucked and applied pressure to my balls with their tongues. OH FUCK, two guys licking balls, one guy sucking my cock and two guys eating heartily at my nipples, I was one lucky so and so that night buds let me tell you all.

"Ohhhhhh man, oh yeah, lick my balls you faggots!" I ranted. "Goin' to cum soon enough…"

I closed my eyes again and enjoyed as the guys worked my feet, my cock and balls *and* my nipples. My head was spinning. After a few more minutes there was no holding it back, I was going to cum, *and I was going to cum like fucking gangbusters!*

"Ohhhhh fuck, ohhhhhh fucking fuck, here it comes you faggots!" I panted breathlessly.

My wussie slave took my cock out of his mouth, held it tight in his hand and stroked it hard as I shot my pent-up giant load.

"OHHHHHRRRR FUCKING A you guys!" I roared, my voice filling the steam filled room. "TOTALLY FUCKING A!"

"Oh yeah Muscle guy, shoot that big sexy load," one of the guys licking my nipples said.

I creamed ropes upon ropes of cum all over my stomach region, onto my Speedo bikini, and even into my wussie slave's hand. It seemed to go on and on and on as the guys kept on licking my balls and sucking real hard at my nipples.

"OOOOOOO GAWD," I whispered in ecstasy.

When I was done my two wussies eagerly licked at all the accumulated cum all over my stomach, sopping it up into their greedy mouths, nothing new there, and sucking it down their throats, as fucking usual. As they ate up my jazz the two guys sucking my nipples began working them harder.

"H-hey, easy with my tits you guys," I said slowly, weakened now. "I'm feelin' all sensitive and sexy here right about now…"

But then, the other guy who had been licking my balls clamped his mouth greedily around my cock and began sucking me like crazy.

"OHHHHHHRRRR no, no," I grunted breathlessly, my mouth opening in shock in the shape of an O, my chin dropping.

"Yeah, fuckin' siphon another load out of him," one of my wussies slaves said happily and defiantly. "Fucking going to work *you* over tonight Big Eddie…"

"FUCK!" I yelled, realizing too late that I had lost control of the situation. "You two wussies will pay for this, turning me into a goddamned sex toy here!"

The two muscular guys sucking my nipples pulled my huge arms behind me and held them there. Soon enough I shot a second load of jazz. The guy sucking me swallowed every fucking drop of it, the greedy fuck, didn't even share the wealth…

"OHHHHHHHHHH yeah, yeah!" I ranted as I sat there shaking in ecstasy.

When I was done again the two guys stopped sucking my nipples and the other guy took my cock out of his mouth. My two wussie slaves were done licking all my cum off my stomach.

"Ohhhhh, what a night this turned out to be," I groaned breathlessly.

"And it's just beginning," one of the guys holding my tired arms said and gave one of my earlobes a suck.

"Wha…" I began.

"Let's take this muscle head to the showers, cool him down a bit, and then work him over in the Jacuzzi *and t*hen in the pool for a while," the other guy holding my other arm suggested.

The guy who had swallowed my second shot of cum held the steam room door open as my two wussies and the two guys helped me down off the top tier. I was weak and breathless as the four of them hoisted me off the floor by my arms and legs and carried me slowly out of the steam room toward the showers.

"Fucking carrying me like I was a sack of laundry," I whispered angrily, the cool air rejuvenating me a bit.

They stood me in a shower stall and as the cool water cascaded over me the two guys stepped in with me and washed me up with liquid soap, paying special attention to my huge chest, my nipples and they even teased me by wedging their soapy fingers in the crack of my ass, cleaning me out back there as well. They laughed when I farted a few times when their fingers were probing me. My cock and balls were hanging seductively and invitingly out of my damned Speedo bikini. Neither of my wussies had thought to pack me back in after I had shot my load two fucking times.

"So, you two are his slaves," the other guy said to my two wussies outside the shower stall.

"You could say that," one of my wussies replied. "Actually we all met through a real estate slash roommate service and we share a big apartment. Eddie, that's the muscle head's name was always parading around the apartment in just those Speedo bikinis of his, showing off that beautiful muscular body that he seemed to work on twenty four hours a day. It felt to us as if he were trying to seduce us."

"Not that we minded," my other wussie chimed in.

"He caught us sniffing his Speedos one night but he didn't seem to mind at all," the first wussie went on. "Instead of us trying to explain ourselves we dropped to our knees in front of him and started worshipping the bikini he was wearing at that moment. Since then we've been his wussie slaves as he likes to call us. He forces us to workout with him and as a reward we get to feast on him…"

"Sounds like a real kinky arrangement to me," the guy standing with my two wussies said. "By the way, my name is Matt."

"I'm Don," my first wussie said and shook hands with Matt.

"I'm Mike," my second wussie said and also shook hands with Matt.

"So he caught you sniffing his Speedos eh?" Matt asked. "Can't say I blame you one bit there guys…"

The two guys washing me down in the shower held my big arms behind me and let the cascading water rinse all the soap from my body. I could have easily pulled out of their grasps at that point as I was feeling pretty revitalized by then, but somehow it was turning out to be an interesting evening so I would let them have their fun with me. Besides, I was about to be sexed over by five fucking horny faggots all at once… When I was all rinsed off they turned off the water and holding my arms, we all stepped out of the shower stall. Matt and my two wussies eagerly ran their hands over my dripping wet god-like body, caressing my huge chest, squeezing and twisting my nipples, and tugging greedily on my big cock, which by the way was hard as a fucking rock, *again*... The two guys holding my arms introduced themselves as Larry and Lester. They were lovers. They were also into threesomes and very kinky experiences. I would fit the bill for them that night. Larry and Lester then each took a tight hold on one of my arms each and meanly stretched them way out at my sides as far as possible.

"AAARHHHHHH!" I roared, wondering at that moment just how smart my decision to allow these guys to have at me really was.

"Work on him you guys," Larry said demandingly. "Like you said earlier in the steam room there's enough of Big Eddie to go around."

My two wussies knelt in front of me and each took one of my big balls into their mouth as Matt knelt behind me and licked the back of my wet Speedo all over.

"Ohhhhhh yeah, yeah," I moaned anew as Larry and Lester stretched my arms more and more.

They were like a human rack the way they were stretching me out...

"Fucking milk his crank again," Lester said to my two wussies.

My two wussies didn't ask for permission to be on my cock, there would be hell to pay when we got home that night. The two wussies took turns sucking my hard cock, tugging on my balls at the same fucking time. Man, what they were all doing to me felt so fucking good at that moment that I didn't want them to ever stop. But then, soon enough I felt the churning in my cock, I was getting ready to cum, *a third fucking time.*

"Ohhhh fuck, ohhhh fucking shit," I rasped and shuddered like mad as I shot my load all over the floor, my wussie Mike holding my cock firmly in his hand.

I shot another goddamned man-sized load of cream and they were all in total awe of it.

"Fuck man, he just shot a load like it was his first one tonight," Larry said, looking at the splattered mess of my cum on the floor.

I hung my head down, breathing hard, panting, and sweating again in their tight grasps...

"Yeah, he always cums like a gusher," my wussie Don said from the floor. "Sometimes we milk him a few times a night, if we've earned it that is..."

"Fuck Muscle head, we're going to have *lots* of fun with you tonight," Lester said and slapped one of my pecs hard after letting go of my arm for a moment.

"OWWWW!" I yelled and my head snapped up.

My two wussies and Matt stood up...

"Let's get him to the Jacuzzi and chow down on those big nipples of his," Larry said. "We can boil him a while and eat his tits at the same time..."

Holding me tight by my arms, Lester and Larry put their other arms around my torso as my two wussies grabbed my long muscular legs. They again hoisted me off the floor, this time carrying me toward the deserted pool and Jacuzzi area. My head lolled back and I was weak again as the four guys carried me, walking slowly. Matt held open the door that led from the shower area to the pool area. The smell of chlorine filled the air as they lowered me carefully into the Jacuzzi, sitting me on the ledge that was under the rapidly gyrating water. The water was hot and gyrated over my chest, the bubbles tickling my erect nipples slightly, which caused those nipples of mine to become even more erect and harder. Under the water a powerful jet stream was driving my ass crack insane. Larry and Lester shucked off their towels and stepped naked into the Jacuzzi, sitting down at my sides, a look of pure lecherousness in their eyes. They each helped themselves to me by squeezing my nipples real hard, twisting them with their thumbs and fingers. That feeling of churning in my cock as my nipples were toyed with set in hard and heavy. I Swear I thought I would shoot another load right under the water of the Jacuzzi as those two faggots played with my nipples and not to mention that I would have shot that load without my giant cock even being touched.

"Ohhhhhhhrrr man," I groaned, my head falling back and forth. "Sooooo fucking hot in here guys..."

My wussie Mike squatted down at my side outside the Jacuzzi, grabbed a handful of my wet hair, gently pulled my head back, and pressed his lips against mine. He kissed me gently and passionately as Larry and Lester helped themselves to the delicacy they craved at the moment, namely my big nipples, sucking, licking and chewing the bejesus out of them. My other wussie, Don, squatted at my other side outside the Jacuzzi and Matt moved my head over to him. He also kissed me gently on the mouth. As my two wussies took turns kissing me Lester and Larry worked my nipples hard with their mouths.

"Ohhhhhhhh, yeah, yeah," I moaned in a real man's passion.

Under the water my cock was hard as a fucking rock all over again but I was hoping that the guys wouldn't make me cum again for a while, *a long while*. I had managed to get control of myself when I thought I would cum without my cock being touched, but trust me buds, it was no easy task, the way those guys were playing suck and slurp with my nipples I could have cum like crazy. When my nipples were hard and painfully pointy Lester and Larry stopped working them and splashed water on them, heating them up, softening them. I saw Matt sitting in front of me in the Jacuzzi and in the daze I was in I could have sworn that he was stroking my cock under the gyrating water, slowly, not enough to make me cum, just enough to keep me on edge and real passive. When my nipples were soft to the touch Larry and Lester again sucked them greedily into their mouths. My two wussies continued kissing me, tonguing my mouth at this point.

"Uhhhhhrrrrhhh," I grunted throatily. "I love you two wussies…"

Don and Mike looked at each other, smiled triumphantly, and kissed and kissed me again…

A while later we were all out of the Jacuzzi. With the temperature of the water so high you can only stay in there for fifteen minutes at a time. I was laying on the side of the Jacuzzi, stretched out on my back, still wearing my navy blue Speedo which just for the record was still pulled down in the front. Larry and Lester were each sucking one of my nipples each; my two wussies were lapping hungrily at my big hairy balls, and Matt, the foot pervert that he was, was licking my feet and sucking my toes. To say it plainly, I was in ecstasy like you would not fucking believe.

"Ohhhhhhrrrrrr yeah, what a fucking night this turned out to be," I whispered huskily. "Fucking horny sons of bitches are feastin' on me like I was a slab of beef…"

Actually, as I lay there being mauled and feasted on that was exactly what I felt like, a slab of beef. As Larry and Lester sucked hard on my nipples they were stroking their hard cocks. So was Matt as he hungrily serviced my big feet. My two wussies knew better than to jack off without my permission. They just kept on sucking, licking, and kissing my balls. A few minutes passed and then Larry and Lester stopped sucking my nipples. They stroked their cocks faster and faster over my chest and then they shot their loads, shooting long ropes of jazz all over my huge chest. They grunted passionately in unison…

I sat up on my elbows and watched as they came and came. Matt wasn't too far behind because he stopped servicing my feet and also stroked his hard cock, over my feet.

"Ohhhh yeah, getting close too now," Matt said breathlessly.

He shot his load all over my goddamned feet, grunting and shaking uncontrollably. His cum felt hot as it slid between my toes and all over the fronts and backs of my feet. Larry pressed a finger against a dry spot on my chest and pushed me back down onto my back.

"Uhhhhhnnn…" I said as I stretched back out on the floor between the Jacuzzi and the pool.

I didn't need three fucking guesses to know what was coming next; I was the fucking buffet after all. Larry and Lester began licking their cum off my chest, sucking hard on my now sore nipples as Matt went to work gobbling down the cum all over my goddamned feet. My two wussies continued servicing my balls. I grunted, groaned and moaned in a real man's passion for the horned guys as they worked me over. They wanted to hear me, they wanted to hear my throes of ecstasy, and they loved making me suffer erotically. My cock was again unbelievably hard, fat, and throbbing with a life all its own, waiting to be made to shoot yet another load. I wondered myself if after having cum three times already I would be able to produce another geyser of jazz. God knew I had almost cum while they had me in the Jacuzzi. A few minutes later the men rolled me into the cool water of the pool. I hit the water with a splash and the five men jumped in after me. They gathered around me, floated me between them, pinched and twisted my nipples, and tugged on my hard cock.

"Mmmmmm…feels so fucking good," I crooned as I floated on the water on my back with my eyes closed, my cock sticking straight up like a flagpole. "Feels real nice…"

They touched and explored me everywhere, not being able it seemed to get enough of my god-like body and then a while later Lester realized just how very late it was. He suggested that we had all better be on our way. Lester, Larry, Matt, and my two wussies climbed out of the pool, leaving me standing in the water, a raging goddamned hard-on between my legs.

"What say we all get dressed and go on back to our place?" Lester said, looking at me hungrily. "I think we can all use further helpings of this uh, hunk…"

"So fucking glad that you volunteered me to be the main course on your menu Fucker," I said with a grin, quickly agreed to Lester's suggestion and swam to the middle of the pool.

I told my two wussies to meet me outside the gym along with the other guys. I told them that I wanted to swim a few good laps to get myself another wind and then I would be outside also. The five guys all dried off and headed for the locker room. I floated around on my back for a few minutes, swam a few laps and then slowly climbed out of the pool, feeling totally rejuvenated and ready for hours of being the main course for these horny faggots. As I was emerging from the pool two gym instructors walked into the pool area from the main entrance.

"I hate having to work the closing," the blond guy was saying as they walked in.

Upon seeing me climbing out of the pool, my raging hard-on in front of me, they stopped in their tracks.

"Uh, sorry," I began. "I guess I didn't realize how late it was. I'll uh, be on my way, my uh, my friends are waiting for me out front…"

Slowly and cautiously the two gym instructors walked over to me, hunger showing in their eyes. My hard cock, embarrassingly on display twitched in front of me, as if beckoning to the two gym instructors. I couldn't believe that after my wussies and the other guys had left me alone in the pool that I hadn't packed myself back into my Speedo.

"Uh, look guys," I said, suddenly feeling very nervous, standing there dripping wet, real sexy and real vulnerable at the same fucking time.

"What's your name guy?" the dark haired instructor asked me, looking ravenously at my nipples.

"Uh, Eddie, my uh, my name is Eddie," I replied, glancing down at my exposed boner and quickly back up at the two gym instructors.

"Well Eddie, it sure is a fucking pleasure to meet you buddy," the blond instructor said slyly. "And your cock…"

"What's up with your man nips Eddie?" the dark haired instructor asked me lustfully. "Looks to me like someone has really been at 'em, big fucking time…"

He reached forward and brazenly gave one of my very sore nipples a squeeze. As he squeezed my nip my hard cock twitched. The way he had called my nipples my man nips sent chills through me for whatever the fuck the reason, causing my exposed cock to twitch some more…

"Yeah, uh, me and a few of my buddies were in the steam room and we were uh, horsing around I suppose you would call it and…" I began saying.

But then, before I even knew what the fuck was happening the two gym instructors were holding my arms behind me and slurping real heartily on my nipples, my newly named man nips. The two fucking guys held me tight and slurped like they were in heated frenzy…

"OHHHHHHHH FUCK, yeah, oh fucking yeah," I moaned. "Here we fucking go again…"

My cock throbbed harder and harder and oozed pre-cum from my wide sexy piss slit.

"Oh man, great fucking man nips Eddie," the blond instructor said. "Is every part of you this fucking delectable and delicious?"

Before I could reply the two instructors stopped slurping on my nipples, grabbed my arms even tighter, twisted them up meanly behind me and began walking me toward the door that they had come in through.

"H-hey, where are we going buds?" I asked them. "ARRRHHHHH, easy with my arms you guys!"

They hustled me quickly upstairs to the deserted gym and before I could stop them they had me tied to a weight bench on my back which was in a semi sitting position.

"Fuckers, what do you guys think you're doing here?" I grumbled, my cock now fear hard in front of me. "Tying me the fuck up? Good God, but the management of this dump will hear about this! I'm a member in good standing at this gym!"

They roped my hands at the wrists behind me and around the back of the weight bench and then they tied each of my big feet to the legs of the bench. The fuckers even gagged me with my bikini and spent the better part of the evening feasting on my nipples, sucking my cock, milking the fuck out of it like crazy, and sucking and suckling every available part of my muscular god-like body…

When I arrived home more than a few hours later my two wussies were awake and waiting for me. I walked in the door wearing blue jeans, a yellow tank top, and high top sneakers, looking utterly and completed wasted and exhausted.

"Master Eddie!" Don said and they both came running over to me. "What happened? Where were you?"

They put their arms around my shoulders and walked me slowly to the bedroom.

"When you didn't come out of the gym we all figured you'd changed your mind and went home, we thought you'd left the gym through the back door," Don went on and I shook my head "no." "But when we got here and saw that you weren't home we had a feeling that something had gone awry. What happened?"

"Oh yeah, something went awry alright, two hornier than all hell gym instructors captured me," I replied breathlessly. "They found me in the pool area after you two and the other guys left me there. Fucking guys got the jump on me, tied me the fuck up in the gym and worked me over like crazy..."

In the bedroom my two wussies helped me out of my tank top and ran their hands over my chest, squeezing my sore nipples, twisting them.

"Guys no, not now...*please...*" I found myself pleading, surprising even to my own ears.

"Who's the wussie now Master Eddie?" Don asked me and slurped hard on one of my nipples.

"You said you loved us back at the gym," Mike said and kissed my other nipple.

"I-I do and I would love you two horned wussies even more if you wouldn't...*oh gods,*" I stammered as they sucked my nipples like crazy.

I put my hands behind their necks as they feasted like two vampires on my nipples. *What a night it had turned out to be...*

■

The Meister

It was a Friday evening when army reserve soldier Timothy Backman would unwittingly become involved in one of the most bizarre police cases the authorities had ever encountered.

"That was a wonderful movie Timmy," Stephanie, Timmy Backman's wife was saying as she and her handsome husband exited the movie theater where they had just enjoyed seeing a classic on the big screen. "I love seeing old-time love stories again and again, especially the ones from when we were dating; it brings back such wonderful memories. I'm so glad my mother was able to take Timmy Junior for a few days. We really deserved some time together this way."

Smiling like a schoolboy, handsome as a leading man, wearing his olive colored reserve soldier dress uniform complete with a tightly knotted necktie and spit shined lace-up patent leather army issued shoes, with his hat tucked under one arm Timmy smiled warmly as his beautiful and sexy wife held tight to his arm as they made their way through the throng of people exiting the theater.

Stephanie could not help but notice how some of the women, the young girls and even some of the guys were taking in the sight of her uniform clad handsome hubby. With a look of satisfaction in her eyes she held tighter to his arm as they walked through the theater lobby. She knew that her handsome husband was really something to behold. There was no mystery there as far as the army wife was concerned.

"Yeah, I'll agree with that Steph," Timmy said, his Southern accent thick. "The movies they make nowadays really can't compare to the ones from our time…but please don't make it sound like we're all that old, I personally would not consider that movie we just saw a classic, maybe in another ten years, but not just yet."

"Well, it was still fun watching it again," Stephanie giggled and held tighter yet to her husband's muscular arm as they walked slowly through the lobby.

"Yes, that is true, it was fun watching it again," Timmy said.

As he spoke Timmy noticed a few cops standing around at the door to the theater box office. When one of the officers spied Timmy in his uniform his eyes were suddenly riveted on the soldier and he started approaching him and Stephanie.

"Say, I wonder what's going on over there," Timmy said and started making his way over to the officer who was approaching him and gesturing at him as well.

"Timmy, I'm sure its nothing, the police can handle it," Stephanie said, wanting more than anything to get home with her handsome reserve soldier and to have him rock her world for an hour or two, or three.

"Sir, I'm Officer Gorshin, may I have a word with you?" the handsome and muscular dark haired cop asked Timmy, smiled at Timmy's wife, tipped his hat at her and held out a meaty hand to shake.

"Uh, sure, I suppose," Timmy replied and shook hands with the cop, the cop then shaking hands with Stephanie. "I'm Timothy Backman, reserve soldier. This is my wife Stephanie. I uh, just got back from my two week duty call, which is why I'm still in uniform that is."

"Well, we sure could use your assistance here Sir," Officer Gorshin said.

"And how can I be of service?" Timmy asked as Stephanie rolled her eyes in her head in disbelief, realizing how it would be a while now before her and her soldier got home.

Stephanie's pussy had been dripping during the love scenes in the movie she and her reserve soldier husband had just sat through and she wanted more than anything to get home to release her pent-up juices and she was sure Timmy felt the same way. But now Timmy was about to become involved in some police case at the movie theater, of all things.

"Well, the theater was robbed during the showing of the movie," the cop replied. "Please follow me to the box office. You see, the gentleman who runs the box office and collects the receipts and cash and credit card slips was the victim. Seems like during the showing of the movie when the theater was quiet was when he was robbed."

"And how would this involve me Sir?" Timmy asked the cop as he followed him toward the box office.

"Well, the gentleman who works in the box office is also a reserve soldier, and his story of what happened during the robbery is astounding to say the least," Officer Gorshin said. "You see, he works here once in a while to help out his buddy who owns the theater. While the movie was in progress a man in a ski mask infiltrated the box office and made off with the earnings from the show you just saw and the two earlier performances as well."

"Oh my word," Timmy said. "And because he's a reserve soldier you want me to check him out?" Timmy asked.

"Well, what we'd like is for you to see if his story of what happened to him sounds plausible," the officer explained. "As I said, it's a bit farfetched, one for the story books so to speak…And judging from the stripes on your arm Sir, you're a major. And the gentleman in the box office stated that he is a captain."

Timmy smiled and followed the officer through the door of the box office. Officer Gorshin introduced Timmy to two other cops, Officer Romero and Office Newmar, Officer Newmar being a sexy looking female cop.

As Stephanie entered the box office with her husband she and the female cop looked at each other and for the briefest of seconds the two women felt their lusty blood boiling. Just as she liked her man in uniform Stephanie secretly liked certain women in uniform as well.

"Uh, Major Backman, this is Captain Hayes," Officer Gorshin said, introducing the two men.

As Stephanie un-clasped her hand from Timmy's arm he took in the sight of the distraught looking young man seated at the desk in the small theater box office. All over the floor were strewn receipts, credit card facsimiles, but no cash was to be seen anywhere. The reserve soldier, who Timmy had been told was a captain looked to be in his mid to upper twenties. He had short cut blond hair and piercing blue eyes. He was casually dressed in blue jeans and a red pull-over Polo shirt. Timmy also quickly noted that the young man was not wearing any kind of footwear, no socks, no shoes, sneakers or even slippers. At the sight of the young man's bare feet Timmy's heart lurched for a moment.

"It's good to meet you Captain Hayes," Timmy said, sounding stern all of a sudden, obviously going into soldier-mode on a subconscious level.

"Sir!" Captain Hayes said and immediately stood on his bare feet. "Major Backman, Sir!"

Even though he was not in uniform he respectfully saluted his superior officer. Timmy saluted in return and then told the young reserve soldier to resume his seat.

"So uh, what's your first name Soldier?" Timmy asked.

"Robert Sir, like the actor, my name is Robert Hayes," the young man responded.

"Okay, good, now, Robert, you want to tell me what happened here?" Timmy asked. "According to Officer Gorshin you were working the box office and you were robbed."

"Y-yes Sir, that's the abridged version of what transpired here," Robert replied and quickly glanced down at his bare feet. "Fucker stole my sneakers and socks too…"

Officer Gorshin and Timmy looked at each other.

"I told you it was an outlandish story, this gets better," the cop said softly so in that the young reserve soldier could not hear him.

"Where do you serve when on reserve duty? Timmy asked Robert.

"Fort Bigelow Sir," Robert replied. "And you Sir?"

"I'm stationed at Fort Hamilton," Timmy replied. "No wonder I don't know you… Okay, on with it then, you were robbed and the assailant also stole your sneakers and socks?"

"Yes Sir," Robert said.

As Timmy and Robert were speaking Stephanie and Officer Newmar were sizing each other up it seemed stealing glances at each other, smiling coyly. The way the two women were teasing each other in such a sexy flirtatious manner was not lost on Officer Newmar's partner, a handsome dark haired, dark eyed Spanish officer named Luis Romero. The muscular cop wondered what it would be like to be the meat in the sandwich between his partner and this sexy woman who was the reserve soldier's wife.

"Why would he uh, steal your sneakers and socks?" Timmy asked Robert, his heart pounding because somehow he knew what the answer would be.

"He said he was going to keep them as a souvenir of this, of having robbed a famous movie theater, of having, of having…"

"Yes? Out with it Soldier, of having what?" Timmy asked.

"Of having tickle tortured me and made me laugh my fool head off while the sad movie was playing in there and while he robbed me…" Robert stated and a hush fell over the small room. "Fucker tickle tortured me Sir…"

Timmy turned to Officer Gorshin and the cop said, "I told you it was an outlandish story Sir."

"Outlandish Officer?" Robert asked, nearly bolting from his seat. "How about the fact that you found me tied up? Hogtied to be exact?"

"We did at that," Officer Gorshin said and looked at Officer Romero.

The Spanish cop held up the plastic evidence bag that contained a few lengths of white cotton rope.

"Could I maybe have a few minutes alone with him?" Timmy asked Officer Gorshin, gesturing toward Robert.

"Sure, but he wasn't able to get a description of the man who he says did this, seeing as the guy was wearing a ski mask," Officer Gorshin said and a few moments later Timmy was sitting in a chair next to his army comrade.

As the young man sipped a glass of water Timmy gently squeezed the back of his neck.

"You okay Captain?" Timmy asked.

"Yes Sir, still feeling a bit winded, the guy took me by surprise and really put me through it," Robert said angrily.

"I'm sure I can relate," Timmy said softly and then bored his eyes into the young man. "Tell me what happened."

"Well Sir, I was sitting in here tallying up the day's receipts, the credit card facsimiles, the cash," Robert began. "And then there was a knock on the door behind me."

"Did you ask who it was?" Timmy asked.

"No Sir, I just figured it was Wayne and I called out "come in", Robert replied.

"Wayne, who is Wayne?" Timmy asked.

"Wayne owns the theater Sir, he's also one of my best friends in the whole world," Robert said. "I help him out here once in a while when it becomes very busy, as it did today."

"I see, and uh, is Wayne the only person who would knock on the door and you would instantly admit in that way?" Timmy asked.

"Well, I never really thought about that Sir, but I suppose you could say so, yes," Robert said.

"Okay, so because you thought it was Wayne at the door you called out "come in" and then what happened?" Timmy asked.

"Well Sir, *he* came in, he was dressed all in black, he was very tall, I would say just about six feet tall, maybe an inch or two more or less, and he had a ski mask over his head, all I could see were his eyes, nose and mouth," Robert said. "At the sight of him I stood up instantly, ready to fend him off. He slammed the door shut and pointed a spray can at me. I swear Sir, I felt like I was suddenly starring in an old fashioned noir movie of some kind."

"My word," Timmy said softly, feeling awful for the young guy.

"Well, anyway Sir, he sprayed the contents of that spray can in my face and it smelled awful, a real sickly sort of scent," Robert went on.

"Aerosolized chloroform," Timmy said through clenched teeth. "DANG, of all things…"

"It made me real sleepy Sir," Robert continued. "I remember falling back into my seat here…and then when I woke up shortly afterwards the bastard had me hogtied on the floor by the desk. He was sitting at the desk and filling a small bag with all the cash I had just tallied for the day. He also took some of the credit card receipts."

"Had he gagged you Soldier?" Timmy asked.

"No Sir, but I didn't take a chance on yelling out, I was thinking he could do worse to me than knock me out with gas, being that he had me all tied the fuck up by then, he was obviously in total control," Robert went on. "When he told me he would be taking my sneakers and white sweat socks as a souvenir of all this was when I realized my feet had been bared. I asked him what the fuck kind of thief steals a guys sneakers and socks. And Sir, Major Backman, his reply was, "this kind of thief" and that was when he started tickle torturing my danged feet. The way my tied feet were sticking straight up he didn't even have to get off the chair to do his damned dirty work."

"Oh my word," Timmy said again and felt his own feet twitching in his army issued shoes.

"Yes Sir, he scribbled his fingertips all over and all over my poor tied up bare feet," Robert stated harshly. "And with all due respect Sir, I'm ticklish as all hell…"

"Yes, I can definitely understand that Robert," Timmy said and crossed one leg on his knee.

"He said he would have me laughing till just about the end of the movie in the theater," Robert said. "And Sir, that movie was only halfway through… While all of you in the theater were sniffling and crying during that danged love story, I was in here being made to laugh till I cried. And Sir, the jist of it all…he filmed it. He had a cam in here and he filmed me laughing and screeching…"

Timmy gripped his black socked ankle and now his heart thundered.

"Why uh, did he say *why* he was tickling you Robert?" Timmy asked.

"Yes Sir, he said he was making a full length tickle epic and that I would be one of his stars in it," Robert said.

"Do you think he came here with the intent of tickling you, like maybe, do you think he saw you working here and came for that reason?" Timmy asked.

"I doubt it Sir, I'm only here once in a while, I think he came with the intent of robbing the theater first and foremost," Robert said. "I think I was sort of what you would call a bonus for him. He did come prepared though, I mean, he had the rope to tie me with and he did have his cam…"

"So obviously he robbed the theater to finance his so called epic, DANG!" Timmy said. "I'm really sorry this happened to you Soldier, and I promise we will get that video back…"

"Ha, if he hasn't made copies of it and started showing it on the internet that is," Robert said angrily. "I tell you Major Backman, Sir, I have never been broken by tickle torture, never, ever, ever. My girlfriend, okay, she tickles me from time to time, we like bondage games, but even when she tickles me she gives up after a while because I just won't laugh. I may be ticklish but I can control myself when the going gets tough. Being a reserve soldier has taught me that. My girlfriend will tease me about how she plans to keep me bound up until I do laugh but when she sees it's futile she backs off. But this guy, oh fuck me Sir, he had a talent for tickling that was unheard of…at least unheard of by me that is Sir…"

"So you've never been made to laugh when being worked over that way?" Timmy asked.

"Well, I wouldn't say never, I mean all guys horse around with tickling, wouldn't you say Sir?" Robert asked.

"I would uh, I would suppose," Timmy replied, his armpits a bit moist and it was at that moment that he realized Robert had his hand on his black socked ankle as he was speaking.

"I uh, I have a buddy who works in a gym as an aerobics instructor Sir," Robert said. "Once in a while I'll meet him at the locker room at the gym when the class he was instructing was done and my workout ended at the same time. Now, look at me Sir, I stand six feet tall, I'm over two hundred pounds of muscle, not exactly a pushover, as you can see. Being a reserve soldier sure keeps a guy in shape, as I'm sure you can attest to. I have two inches and fifty pounds on this buddy of mine that I'm telling you about. Once, he took about ten to fifteen seconds worth of tickle jabs at me. I'll tell you Major Backman, this guy could have been a boxer, and he was that good, that danged fast. I reacted and tried to block him but he would land two more shots just as I was still blocking his first onslaught. He told me I was all nerves and he laughed at my situation as I kept backing into a row of lockers. Big as I am, strong like a bull, there was not much I could do about it. I mean, it's not like I'll fight a guy smaller than me, and definitely not a friend pulling a prank. But I could not get near him to tickle him, he had taken me totally by surprise, just as whoever it was today had done, taken my totally by surprise, with that damned stinking gas he made me inhale, fuck! But my buddy in the locker room, I could not get near enough to tickle jab him back. Each time I moved toward him he would tickle my ribs or even manage to squiggle a finger or two in my armpits and while I was laughing my head off I would be trying to stop him yet again…"

When he was done speaking Robert squeezed Timmy's black socked ankle, snapped the elastic in his sock against his skin and then took his hand away. Timmy felt a definite churning in his cock, for various reasons the reserve soldier realized.

"Okay Soldier, again, I'm sorry this happened to you, but thank God whoever the assailant was didn't hurt you, or worse," Timmy said and stood up.

"Worse Sir?" Robert asked as Timmy headed to the door of the office to readmit the police officers. "He gassed me into a stupor, he tied me up, he tickle tortured and robbed me and he stole my sneakers and socks. How could it have been worse?"

Timmy, thinking about a man named Ronald Greene said, "He could have kidnapped you Soldier, he could have kidnapped you and tickle tortured you for days on end…"

As Officers Gorshin, Romero and Newmar made their way back into the office along with Timmy's wife Stephanie the young reserve soldier gulped hard in terror at what Timmy had just said to him…

"Everything okay in here?" Officer Gorshin asked Timmy.

"As well as can be expected Officer," Timmy replied, reaching into his uniform jacket pocket and producing a business card. "Take this, and keep me posted on this case."

"Yes Sir, may I ask why?" Officer Gorshin asked, looking at Timmy's name and phone number on the card.

"I have a feeling that my fellow reserve soldier here will not be the last in this sort of robbery scenario," Timmy replied glum faced. "I have a feeling, being that the assailant filmed himself tickling Robert here that he will be doing this to other people down the line. I also think he's done it before today…just that it did not get reported…"

"Okay Sir, if I hear of another case like this I will summon you for sure," Officer Gorshin replied, a look of incredulousness on his face. "Never heard of a case though where the robbery victim was tickle tortured…"

"Well now you have," Timmy said and looked at Robert once more. "Tell me Robert, did the man in the ski mask tell you his name by any chance?"

Robert looked up at his superior officer and said, "While I was laughing and begging him to stop tickling me he told me to call him "The Meister."

"The Meister?" the sexy female cop, Officer Newmar asked.

"Yes Maam, he said he was "The Tickle Meister." Robert replied. "He said to beg the "Tickle Meister" to stop tickling me. So I did, I begged, I roared at him, "please Tickle Meister, stop tickling me!" But he didn't, at least not till I had really laughed till I cried to his satisfaction."

"Officer Gorshin, please get a final statement from Captain Hayes here and then finish up your report," Timmy said to the cop who was obviously in charge. "I'll file a report with the captain's commanding officer as well. He may want Robert checked out medically because he was drugged with chloroform. I'm sure he's okay but it is procedure after all. I myself am not a stranger to chloroform I'm sad to say… Oh, and please supply Robert with some shoes and socks. You can charge it to his commanding officer. If there are any questions you can direct him or her to call me. And please keep in touch with me as well."

"Yes Sir Major Backman, and thank you so much for your time," Officer Gorshin said and Timmy and Stephanie politely made their exit, Stephanie and Officer Newmar smiling a knowing and wicked smile at each other.

"The guy was robbed *and* tickle tortured?" Stephanie asked Timmy as they exited the movie theater.

"Yeah, can you believe that?" Timmy asked, straightening his tie, even though it didn't need straightening at that moment.

Timmy had to think how his lovely wife had no idea whatsoever that he himself was once a tickle victim, a kidnapped tickle victim to be exact.

"I hate to say this but it sounds like something that author buddy of yours, Christopher Trevor would write about," Stephanie said as they headed for their car.

"Sure as hell does," Timmy said. "It could somehow be good fodder for him for an upcoming book, if he's interested that is. I mean, as bad as I feel for Captain Hayes back there Christopher could very well turn this negative into a positive. And seeing as I invited him to the reunion of me and my military buddies in a few days that's where I suppose I'll tell him about this…and any other cases that may happen between now and then."

As they settled into the car, Timmy in the driver's seat, Stephanie in the passenger seat, she said, "You really think this will happen again, and so soon at that?"

"Somehow I'm sure of it babe," Timmy said pressed his foot to the gas pedal.

As he drove Timmy thought of what Officer Gorshin had said at the outset of their meeting back in the theater, about finding out if Captain Hayes' story was plausible sounding. To Timmy, to someone who had been in numerous tickle traps it sounded totally plausible. Timmy Backman knew that there were men out there and some women as well, who thrived on driving a poor captured guy crazy with tickle tortures…and poor Captain Hayes had just fallen victim to a new tickle villain it seemed. Timmy gripped the steering wheel tight and whispered the words, "Tickle Meister…"

The next day, Saturday afternoon, Officers Gorshin and Romero found themselves being interrogated by their sergeant, a hulking figure of a muscle brute named Sergeant James Russo to be exact. Sergeant Russo barely fit into his navy blue police uniform. It was said around headquarters that the man was so muscular that they did not make uniforms in his size, hence the reason he always seemed to be bulging out of it…and in all the right places at that it seemed. Officer Romero, a man who loved the ladies, and at the moment especially that reserve soldier's wife, Stephanie Backman, had to admit that the way the sergeant's big nipple tips were pressing against his uniform shirt and making a nice impression was making him salivate. Officer Romero loved sucking and servicing a good pair of tits, and whether they were man tits or lady tits did not make a difference to the Spanish cop, in his opinion tits was tits…

"I'm not understanding this report gentlemen," Sergeant Russo said, holding up the paperwork submitted by the two cops in his office. "And where is Officer Newmar at the moment? Wasn't she involved in this case as well?"

It uh, it's her day off today Sir," Officer Gorshin said.

"Okay, so it is," the sergeant went on. "But please continue here, seeing as you two can probably fill me in on all I need to know. Tell me why a guy made his way into a movie theater disguised in a ski mask and made off with only less than a few grand. It just doesn't make a whole lot of sense to me. It would seem like the robbery was a cover-up for something else, something bigger perhaps…"

"Well Sir, if you read the entire report you see that the victim, the guy working the box office was also terrorized, he was gassed, tied up and uh, tickled, he was tickle tortured and the assailant caught it all on video," Officer Gorshin said. "That video is out there somewhere Sir. And the guy captured on it and humiliated is a reserve soldier in the United States army. The reserve soldier also said that the guy who tickled and filmed him said something about making a tickle epic film. So it does look like the robbery was a cover-up, of sorts. I think you are correct that it's all part of something bigger…"

"Yes, tickle tortured and filmed, of all things," the sergeant said and in a supposedly subconscious manner trailed a wide open hand over his nipples areas. "And as luck would have it, this Major Timothy Backman just happened to be at the theater with his wife that afternoon."

"Yes Sir, with his wife," Officer Romero said, the expression on his face telling a story.

"Yes, when I saw him I figured it would be best to have him interview the victim, seeing as they are both reserve soldiers," Officer Gorshin said.

"I suppose that was a good idea Officer Gorshin, I think Major Backman may have garnered us more information than we would have gotten had he not been there. I am not diminishing your intelligence please understand. Just that I am sure being that Major Backman is a reserve soldier like our victim is made him open up a bit more."

"Yes Sir, my thoughts exactly," Officer Gorshin said, not aware that Officer Romero was now staring fixedly at his sergeant's nipples as they pressed against his uniform shirt, his staring not lost on the sergeant who grinned fiendishly for a moment.

"Now, the victim, Captain Robert Hayes said the man who assaulted him called himself "The Tickle Meister?" the sergeant asked, looking at the last page of the report.

"Yes Sir," Officers Gorshin and Romero said in unison.

"And according to Major Backman he will strike again, so in other words we are going to be dealing with a serial tickler?" the sergeant asked with a grin.

At that the three men laughed a bit.

"As funny as it sounds, yes Sir, and for some people out there who are hyper sensitive, tickling can become true torture," Officer Gorshin said.

"Care to elaborate on that a bit Officer?" Sergeant Russo prodded.

"Well, sure Sir, a tied up person may be laughing crazily as they're tickle tortured in whatever are their most sensitive regions, stomach area, ribs, armpits, and for most ticklish people the bottoms of the feet being the most horrendous," Officer Gorshin stated. "But even though the person is laughing they really are not having a good time. Uncontrollable laughter really is the only reaction most ticklish tickle victims can produce. So in a way it's a double edged sword Sir..."

The sergeant seemed to contemplate this and then said, "Seems to me you're experienced in this area Officer?" Officer Gorshin smiled a bit coyly and said, "I'm very ticklish Sir, so I know that I would not want to be made to laugh my head off..."

Again all three of the men in the office laughed a bit...

A few moments later Officer Gorshin exited the sergeant's office while Officer Romero was ordered to stay behind for some more official business... Officer Gorshin, unbeknownst to Officer Romero and Sergeant Russo knew all about the trysts the two men enjoyed with each other every once in a while... he knew what the "official business" really entailed...

While Sergeant Russo was interrogating the two officers based on their report from the previous day Officer Newmar was at that moment arriving at Timmy and Stephanie Backman's home. Stephanie Backman, glad that she had sent her son, Timmy Junior, off with her mother for a few days and also glad that her handsome husband was spending time at the base on army reserve duty, sat down to relax with her last cup of morning coffee before dressing for a shopping trip. She was still wearing Timmy's favorite Victoria's Secret nightgown and sheer wispy little housecoat. She leaned back in Timmy's big leather chair and propped her feet on the ottoman, admiring her manicured toes as she sipped the rich, black, vanilla bean tea. Stephanie sighed in total comfort, thinking of the night before, how Timmy's cock had been at better than full mast as she rode him. It seemed that somehow the case of the reserve soldier who worked at the movie theater having been robbed and tickle tortured had really gotten to her handsome sexy husband. Her pussy was still feeling the after-effects of the nearly all night long fuck session her own reserve soldier had subjected her to, not that she was complaining she thought as she sipped her coffee. As she leaned back further in the chair she heard a knock at the front door.

"Now who in the hell could that be?" Stephanie mumbled to herself. "Timmy is long gone for the day to meet his army obligation and Mom has Timmy Junior with her. I'm not expecting anyone else."

Stephanie opened the door a crack and her mouth dropped open when she saw a tall sexy policewoman in full uniform standing on her doorstep. It was Officer Newmar from the night before at the movie theater. Stephanie recalled how they had been sizing each other up while Timmy and the male officers were dealing with the tickled and robbed Captain Hayes. Stephanie took in the fact that this policewoman had to be at least six feet tall, as compared to her own height of five feet eight. The uniform the policewoman was wearing was tight…actually, it was nearly formfitting, leaving very little to imagine about the shape of this statuesque beauty. The policewoman removed her hat and placed it beneath one arm. She also removed her mirrored sunglasses and hung them from her tight shirt pocket, which was pressed outward because of her obviously large breasts beneath. The officer's hair was pulled tightly back into a bun, giving her a strong, almost sexy masculine aura. But, there was nothing masculine about the long angular shape of this obviously sexy woman standing before Stephanie.

As Stephanie took in this almost Amazonian beauty standing here she again took note of the nametag, Newmar. This was most definitely the tall striking policewoman that she and Timmy had seen at the ticklish crime scene the night before. Now, not only was Stephanie's mouth hanging open, but her hand fell to her side and her flimsy little housecoat fell open to reveal her sexy little nightgown beneath. The officer smiled and stuck out her hand.

"Mrs. Backman, I'm Officer Newmar of the police department," the female cop said. "We met last night at the crime scene, at the movie theater."

Officer Newmar took Stephanie's hand and shook it in greeting, which caused the seemingly stupefied housewife to vibrate allover. Her housecoat ever so gently was slipping off her shoulders and sliding down her arms. Officer Newmar licked her lips at the sight of the sexy housewife standing there in her next to nothing nightgown and wispy and now covering nothing housecoat. Enjoying the view of Stephanie's cleavage and milky soft neck and shoulders, and not to mention her long bare legs and feet, Officer Newmar pushed past the housewife and into the warm and cozy home.

"May I come in?" she asked as her arm below her short sleeved uniform shirt brushed against Stephanie's hardening nipples.

"Why, uh, yes!" Stephanie agreed and closed the door.

Then, Stephanie could see the officer's high firm ass moving in the tight blue uniform pants.

"My, my…" she mumbled as she continued to admire the sleek, well proportioned and obviously voluptuous woman who was now gracing her living room. "To uh, to what do I owe the pleasure of your visit to my home, Officer Newmar?"

Officer Newmar turned once more to face Stephanie and pulled her pen and pad from her shiny leather belt. She placed her hat on the nearest end table.

"That is correct Mrs. Backman, I am Officer Newmar, Judy Newmar," the female cop said, almost cooing. "But please, think of me as a friend and just call me Judy. We really don't need the formalities of you as a civilian and me as a police officer."

As the female police officer was speaking she seemed to drink in Stephanie's sexy beauty, which was all but on display beneath her flimsy little costume.

"I came here today because I wanted to get some more insight into what information you might have had about last night's criminal activity involving this tickle fiend…the tickle Meister."

Stephanie moved toward the officer as she responded, "Well, actually it's my husband, Timmy Backman who is involved in that case and he would be the one with any information. But he's not here…he's gone to his army reserve unit. May I uh, offer you some coffee?"

Stephanie smiled as she awaited the officer's reply. Stephanie had yet to readjust her little housecoat, which hung at her elbows, much like a shawl.

"Ah, so that handsome soldier boy husband of yours if off at his reserve soldier thing yes?" the female cop, questioned as she tossed her pen and pad into her hat on the nearby table. "I'm sorry to hear that you don't know more to assist in my investigation."

"Yes, my husband, Timmy, he's completing his reserve soldier thing at the base this weekend," Stephanie said, her lips quivering now.

"Well, I do think I will have that cup of coffee," Officer Newmar said. "And then you can tell me about your stunning sleepwear. I do believe that that is the sexiest thing I have ever seen."

Stephanie realized that the officer was becoming a bit forward, the cop's eyes were twinkling and her tongue was darting across her lips. Stephanie moved over to the bar where her coffee pot rested.

"This little thing, why, Timmy bought this for me at Victoria's Secret," Stephanie said shyly. "Do you take cream and sugar in your coffee?"

The officer followed Stephanie over to the bar and moved up behind her as she poured the coffee. Putting her hands on Stephanie's upper arms and almost whispering in Stephanie's ear she said, "In your presence, who needs sugar?" and she squeezed the housewife's shoulders, causing the housecoat to finally fall to the floor. Stephanie moaned and put the coffee pot down, avoiding a spill. The officer then moved her hands to Stephanie's shoulders and slid the tiny strap off…and the filmy little top fluttered to the floor, piling on top of her housecoat.

Stephanie did not resist the officer's advances and her eyes were closed and she was breathing deeply through her mouth. Officer Newmar slid her hands down Stephanie's bare arms and hooked her thumbs in the tiny little flimsy thong, the only thing Stephanie was still wearing. Her thumbs stretched the material and pushed it over the hump of Stephanie's exquisite bottom… reaching her thighs, it too fell into the little pile at Stephanie's beautiful bare feet.

Stephanie was completely naked, Officer Newmar had so quickly and efficiently stripped the beautiful housewife of her little, hardly anything Victoria's Secret outfit. Stephanie shivered and jumped then as Officer Newmar pressed herself against the naked housewife.

"OOO, your badge is cold!" Stephanie shuddered.

Then, Stephanie turned to face the taller, sexy female police officer. Grasping the officer's patent leather utility belt, Stephanie added, "You do have me at a bit of a disadvantage, don't you think?" and she removed the officer's heavy belt, holding the gun, cuffs, radio and a couple of other pouches.

Officer Newmar did nothing to interfere with Stephanie's actions. She just looked on longingly as Stephanie wrapped the heavy leather belt around her own naked hips, giving her an unusual and kinky appearance. Stephanie's eyes twinkled as she shifted her hips, making the equipment jiggle and sway on the belt…not to mention her full firm breasts, now facing the officer.

"You know, I've never worn a policewoman's uniform," Stephanie said and she proceeded to unbutton the officer's blue blouse, pulling it from her trousers. Officer Newmar watched the housewife work and enjoyed the sway and jiggle of her naked breasts as she unbuckled her belt, unfastened her trousers and lowered the zipper. Stephanie pushed the dark uniform pants down over the officer's ample hips and buttocks.

The policewoman's pants slid down her shapely legs and gathered at her ankles as Stephanie pushed the blouse off her shoulders. Then, Stephanie leaned in nibbling on Officer Newmar's neck as she moved around behind the female cop, pulling the blouse off her extended arms. Feeling Stephanie kiss and nibble on her neck and shoulder, Officer Newmar closed her eyes and moaned at the pleasurable touches of the sexy housewife…but, there was something cold on her wrists…and…"CLICK." The female cop's eyes popped open, as she realized that her own handcuffs were now snapped around her wrists, pinning her arms behind her.

"What do you think you're doing Stephanie Backman?" the officer asked in her in charge voice as she felt the clasp of her bra loosen and snap free and then the straps being pulled off her shoulders and slinking down to tangle with the cuffs at her wrists.

Stephanie then leaned in…her full hot breasts pressing against the officer's back. She whispered, "I'm playing cops and robbers…and you're under arrest Officer Newmar." Stephanie giggled and she reached down and pushed the officer's thong past her ass. Now, except for her black socks and patrol Oxfords, the statuesque Officer Newmar was now as naked as Stephanie, the beautiful and voluptuous housewife. But, right now Stephanie seemed to control the situation and she pushed the taller officer over to the couch. She then pushed the female cop facedown on the cushions.

"Now, Officer Newmar, no…that's too formal," Stephanie said. "What was your first name again?"

As Stephanie teasingly asked the female cop her name, knowing it was Judy, she stripped the tangle of trousers and underpants from the officer's ankles and tossed them casually away.

"My name is Judy, Judy Newmar, I told you that earlier Mrs. Backman," stuttered the now subdued officer.

"Judy, ah yes, okay, Judy it is," Stephanie said, then sitting on the small of the taller woman's back and pinning her cuffed wrists right at the crack of her ass, Stephanie started rummaging through the equipment pouches on the patrol belt.

"Ah, ha," Stephanie said as she found and extracted some of the plastic cuffs, originally made for the electrical industry, but transformed into cheap quick cuffs by law enforcement.

Pushing the female cop's socks down, Stephanie pulled one of the plastic bands around her ankles and pulled it tight. Stephanie then looped one through the metal handcuffs and pulling the officer's feet up and back toward her wrists she secured a third band between the two bands already in place, thereby placing the officer in a hogtied position…

"What are you doing?" Officer Newmar demanded.

In response Stephanie simply laughed her throaty, sexy laugh.

"I think you came here with the idea of having fun…and that's what I'm going to do, have fun," Stephanie said. "The way you and I were looking at each other at the movie theater last night told me all I needed to know, and then you showed up here. Good thing my husband gave your partner, Officer Gorshin all our information, including our home address, yes Officer Newmar?"

With that, Stephanie began pulling the shoestring on the officer's patrol oxfords.

"Yes, yes…I did come here to have fun, but as you just said, I thought you and I had made contact," the female cop blubbered. "Why are you being so deliberate with my shoes Mrs. Backman?"

Officer Newmar, already naked, but the way Stephanie had hogtied her and the way she was being deliberately slow, teasingly slow, with pulling on her shoestrings, this worried Officer Judy Newmar. Having sex with this sexy housewife was one thing, but the way she as going at her, DAMN, the cop realized she hadn't thought about how ticklish her feet were. Surely, Stephanie, Mrs. Backman, didn't have any ideas about tickling her big sexy ticklish feet the cop was thinking. Her shoes were now off her feet and Stephanie was pulling on the cop's black socks, but she didn't just pull, she was…

"Hee, hee, hee…" Mrs. Backman, Stephanie, don't do, hee, hee, hee, hee…you're tickling my feet, hee, hee, hee…" Officer Newmar suddenly found herself saying and laughing.

And then the cop felt the cool air caress her toes as her socks disappeared from her feet.

"OOOO, somebody is ticklish on her feeties," Stephanie taunted as she played her fingernails up and down the upturned wrinkled soles of the statuesque but hogtied police officer. Judy Newmar was now the hogtied captive of the sexy woman that she had intended on seducing and ravishing with her mouth… And Stephanie would tickle Officer Newmar till she lost consciousness the devilish housewife was thinking…

Sometime later, Officer Newmar awoke from her tickle and oxygen deprived sleep to find she was still naked but free from her previous bonds. Freed, but, being hugged and caressed by the equally naked housewife. Stephanie cradled the statuesque woman in her arms and kissed her on her forehead and stroked the female officer's large breasts. As Officer Newmar came out of her unconscious state, she quickly became aware of the abundant sexual longing that had been initially tapped by when she came into Stephanie's home, but, had been piqued by the stripping and tickling by the lusty housewife.

So, with lust burning in her loins, Officer Judy Newmar reached for Stephanie's head and drew her face close to her own…lips parted and mouths quickly ground together…tongues darted and fought for control… neither wanting to win or lose this battle, but just to continue the battle. Judy Newmar's hands explored Stephanie's body, and rose, pushing the housewife back onto the couch. Hard nipples poked at each other and two sets of full, firm breasts pressed together. Then, Officer Newmar spun herself into a sixty-nine position; straddling Stephanie's face…and buried her own face into the sexy housewife's crotch. The cop's tongue lavishly raped Stephanie's shaved snatch. Encouraged by the officer's lips and tongue Stephanie returned the favor. Now, with her reserve soldier husband busy with his duties and this case of the tickle fiend he had been thrust into the night before…and with Officer Newmar off duty this would be a glorious and erotic lesbian love-fest and feast Stephanie thought. A love feast filled with lapping, licking, sucking, slurping and anything else the two women could dream up to do to each other…and just as they were doing just that and not resisting each other…

Officer Romero was not resisting Sergeant Russo's orders to service his huge nipples at the same time in his locked office at police headquarters.

Officer Romero's wrists were locked behind him in his own handcuffs and he was on his knees in front of the sergeant as the muscular man leaned forward his bare chest and served his nipples to the officer...

"And when will your soldier be home Mrs. Backman?" Officer Newmar asked Stephanie, once she was able to pry her lips off her mouth.

"Not, not till tonight," Stephanie replied breathlessly as the female cop tweaked her nipples under her blouse. "Oh Yes, yes, my nipples, work my nipples Officer..."

While Stephanie was engaging in an afternoon tête-à-tête with Officer Newmar and while Officer Gorshin waited for his partner to finish up with Sergeant Russo, a man named Adam, or more poetically known as "The Tickle Meister" was making ready for his next robbery/tickle victim filming...

"You really think this place is a good location?" one of the two men who had teamed up with the tickle Meister asked as their van pulled up in the back entrance of a huge bakery that was located on the west side of Manhattan in New York City.

Like the movie theater that the tickle Meister had robbed the previous day this bakery was just about world famous. Many a celebrity's wedding planner had had the cake made in this bakery. Many a wealthy socialite had had their party catered with sweets from the famed and celebrated establishment. It was not a bakery that catered to the average store. Cakes, pies, cookies and all other sorts of creative confections had to be mail ordered or as time had marched on internet ordered from the esteemed enterprise.

"It's a perfect location, I did some research on this place," the tickle Meister said jovially. "The only people here on a Saturday afternoon are the bakers, two women and two men to be exact and one security guard. Most of the other staff does not work on Saturday's. They have a revolving schedule for weekend work. We going in there disguised as delivery men will give us total access to the place."

"You plan on tickling another chicken for your video?" the second man asked the tickle Meister as they all stepped out of the van.

"Why I have to be asked such unbelievable and stupid questions is beyond me," the tickle Meister said, donning a chef's hat and a pair of geeky looking eyeglasses. "How many times must I explain to you two that this is all a rouse, a red herring for the author Christopher Trevor, a chance to finally see that sadistic author get the tables turned on him? He has tickle tortured so many men in his tales, and some women too if I recall correctly. In other books he has spanked unwitting and burly men. Once he's been brought into the loop where this ongoing tickle rant that I'm on is concerned I'm sure he will not be able to resist writing about it. And I plan to give him firsthand knowledge on being tickled to the point of insanity…and spanked as well, perhaps, so yes, I am sure there will be a worthy ticklish victim within these walls for me to add to my growing epic film. The security guard will due nicely…"

"Why the security guard and not one of the bakers who work in there?" the first man asked.

"We won't be going anywhere near the bakers, we will be encountering only the security guard, and his post is near the vault where the bakeries earnings are stored," the tickle Meister said. "The vault is emptied every Wednesday via armored car. And last week they did not have a cash pickup, seemed there was some sort of discrepancy in the books. The owners wanted to wait for the accounting department to solve the error and then they would arrange a cash pickup and have it deposited in their bank. So I'm guessing that there should be a hefty haul in there right about now. It will be the perfect scene, just as the one at the movie theater was."

The tickle Meister reached into his pocket and held up a long goose feather. He and his two Cohorts looked at the feather as the man known as the tickle Meister whispered the name "Christopher Trevor." Then, he slid the feather back into his pocket and pointed at the back of the van…

"At least this time we get to participate in the tickling," the first man said.

"Yes Clyde, you and James should thoroughly enjoy this scene," the tickle Meister stated as he straightened his chef's hat atop his head and tried to look as dumb as possible behind the geeky looking glasses he had donned.

A few short minutes later a college aged security guard posted in the backroom of the huge bakery on the west side of Manhattan was instantly on his feet and standing blocking the way as the tickle Meister and his two Cohorts entered the establishment. The scents of fresh pies, cakes and cookies wafted around and filled the huge area. The security guard, a blond towheaded young guy of approximately twenty years old, with brown eyes stood with his palm raised. At the sight of him in his navy blue and black uniform complete with a tightly knotted necktie, black patent leather lace-up shoes and no doubt dark colored silk dress socks the tickle Meister's eyes lit up.

"Excuse me, but you three can't come in here," the security guard, whose nametag pinned to his uniform shirt read "Stu" said.

Stu quickly noted that two of the men were carrying square boxes, pie boxes to be exact, while the third had a video cam in hand, and blast it all he was filming their entrance it seemed…it also seemed that he himself was being filmed as well.

"Why can't we come in here? Explain yourself my good man," the tickle Meister said demandingly yet with a grin of pure lust on his face as the young man named Stu blocked their way.

"Well, first of all the place is closed on Saturday and second of all it's the rules," Stu said and then turned to the man with the cam. "And please turn off that camera Sir, I do not like that that thing is pointed in my direction."

"You're doing fine, just fine," the tickle Meister's cohort, James, with the camera deadpanned.

The tickle Meister took in the fact that the security guard was not armed and opened the box he was carrying. He also took in the fact that the safe with the bakeries weekly earnings was directly across from the security guard's station…

"But alas we are deliverymen my good man," the Meister stated and as Stu watched he took a thickly creamed pie from the box and held it aloft on the palm of an open hand. "And the bakers here are expecting us. We have these sweets to deliver for them to work their magic on…"

"What all are you going on about Mister?" Stu asked the Meister. "Magic my feet, the bakers here create their own confections, they do not, I repeat, *do not* get anything from the outside…"

"Your feet is right my dear man, for you see these confections are special in many ways, especially the secret ingredient in the creamy thick frosting you are currently feasting your eyes on," the Meister said jovially. "For this cream has been known to cure insomnia…"

The tickle Meister's cohort, James, was now standing off to the side catching this moment all on film as he aimed his cam at the security guard.

"Cure insomnia?" Stu asked. "Now how in all hell could a creamy frosting do that?"

"Like this!" the Meister said loudly, his voice echoing and booming off the walls and while the security guard was momentarily startled the Meister threw the heavy creamed pie, aiming it directly at the security guard's face.

"PWAHHHHHHH!" Stu ranted, his cap flew off his head and instantly his fingers were scratching at his face, trying to get the cream that he had been splattered with off, the mess of it dripping down onto his uniform shirt and tie.

The Meister laughed insanely and said, "POW, right in the kisser!" and watched as the security guard danced stupidly and was slowly being sent off to dreamland.

"WH-what all is happenin' here?" Stu asked dumbly as his head spun.

Some of the cream slopped to the floor and Stu found himself sliding perilously around in it, his shoes being leather soled...

"As I told you my good man, these pies cure sleeplessness," the Meister laughed and gestured toward his cohort, Clyde, who was holding the other box containing a second pie.

As James captured the pied in the face security guard's dancing and rantings Clyde lifted a second pie from his box.

"Look over here mine little birdie," Clyde chuckled and Stu, unwittingly did just that.

The Meister grabbed the young man's upper arm, held him steady and Stu's eyes bugged wide open within the mess of cream adorning his features. Before he could duck or move out of the way he saw a second cream pie headed for his face.

"PWAHHHHHHHH!" Stu ranted a second time.

"HA, right in the puss!" the Meister laughed and let go of Stu's arm.

The security guard inhaled the chloroform that was laced into the cream and buckled to the floor...

"Okay, one of you start working the safe, the other help me with the kid," the Meister said. "And set up that cam so we're all seen tickling him..."

"Yes Sir!" the Meister's cohorts called out heartily and in unison.

Timmy Backman was driving home from Fort Hamilton early that evening when his cell phone rang. He pulled it from his uniform jacket pocket, flipped it open, saw that it was a number he did not know and held it to his ear.

"Backman here," Timmy said.

"Major Backman, its Officer Gorshin calling," Timmy heard the cop saying. "Seems we have another robbery and another tickle victim as well.'

"Is he another reserve soldier?" Timmy asked, slowing his car down.

"No Sir, but he is a security guard," the cop said. "I realize I'm imposing on you a bit here Sir, but you did have a lot of luck talking with the victim at the movie theater and..."

"Where should I meet you?" Timmy asked, cutting the cop off in mid sentence.

"The Arlington Bakery, do you know where it is?" Officer Gorshin asked the reserve soldier.

"Sure, who doesn't know where that bakery is?" Timmy asked. "You mean to tell me the tickle Meister robbed a bakery?"

"Sure as all hell he did Major Backman," the cop said.

"Okay, I'll meet you there," Timmy replied.

"Back entrance Major Backman, he got in that way," the cop said and he and Timmy hung up.

Timmy speed dialed his home number and told Stephanie that there had been another robbery and tickling, adding that he would be aiding Officer Gorshin again.

"After I'm done I'll be on my way home babe," Timmy said lovingly.

"Sure Timmy, that's fine, after all, no one knows more about tickling than you," Stephanie said, sounding sexy as all hell.

"Sadly in a way that is true babe," Timmy said and hung up his cell phone again.

"Good thing he called eh?" Officer Newmar asked Stephanie as her face dangled over Timmy's wife's moist and much eaten pussy.

"Yes, you could say that, now, we have a little time left, so please, please..." Stephanie purred.

The female cop grinned, hoisted Stephanie's thighs slightly upward and plunged her tongue into Stephanie's pussy for what seemed like the umpteenth time that day. Stephanie moaned contentedly...

After hanging up with his wife Timmy Backman, clad in full uniform made his way to the Arlington bakery...

He pulled up behind the parked police cruiser and stepped out of his car, unaware that in a nearby van a cam was pointed at him through a peephole...

"Why would a soldier be making the scene Adam?" James asked the tickle Meister as he filmed Timmy's arrival.

"I don't know, let me take a look," the Meister said, momentarily stopping the counting of the cash that he and his two cohorts had purloined from the bakery's vault.

The Meister looked out the small window of the van, saw Timmy entering the bakery via the back entrance and whispered the name "Christopher Trevor" yet again.

"But that's not the author," James said as he turned off the cam.

"No, but it's one of his main characters in the flesh," the Meister said. "This is becoming juicier and juicier I must say…"

The Meister held up a pair of patent leather lace-up shoes with a pair of navy blue dress socks sticking out of them. He whispered the name "Stu."

"So you think that that soldier can lead us to Christopher Trevor?" James asked.

"Yes, and much quicker than in the way I had originally planned on," the Meister said with a grin.

At that the van pulled away…

As Timmy entered the back entrance of the famous Arlington bakery he was greeted by the sight of Officers Gorshin and Romero, a forced open vault and a distraught looking handsome security guard. The security guard was seated on a chair, his face held the remnants of what looked like creamy frosting and his uniform shirt and pants looked to be riddled with what appeared to be some sort of sticky wrapping paper. Like Captain Robert Hayes at the movie theater his feet were bare, no shoes or socks. Timmy didn't need three guesses to know what had become of the security guard's shoes and socks.

"Major Backman thanks for coming," Officer Gorshin said, approaching the reserve soldier with his palm open and outstretched.

"Not a problem Officer Gorshin, seems like I'm really involved in all this at this point, two tickle victims in two days," Timmy said and saw how the security guard looked up at him miserably. "So, what do we have here? Looks like the vault was robbed…"

"That's for sure," Stu piped up, sounding angry as all hell. "Fuckers took me totally by surprise. And what do you mean two victims in two days Soldier boy?"

Timmy could tell that this victim was not going to be as polite and respectful as Captain Robert Hayes had been…

"By the way Major, the owners of the bakery are on their way here now," Officer Gorshin informed Timmy.

Timmy nodded and returned his attention to the security guard…

"Why are you here Soldier boy?" Stu asked Timmy. "Is the bakery at war or something?"

"Not at all Sir, can we uh, can we begin with your name?" Timmy asked.

"Sure, I'm Stu, Stu Parker," the security guard replied.

"Good to meet you Stu, I'm reserve soldier Major Timothy Backman," Timmy said and held out his hand.

The security guard reluctantly took Timmy's hand in his and shook it.

"Good to meet you too Soldier boy," Stu said and let go of Timmy's hand.

"Have you told the officers what transpired here Stu?" Timmy asked the security guard.

"You mean did I tell them that I was pied in the face twice with pies that had cream in them that was laced with chloroform?" Stu asked Timmy sarcastically. "Did I tell them that the bakery's vault was robbed on my watch? Fuckers used some kind of mild explosive to blow the vault open, damn! Did I tell the officers that the thugs rolled me up in packaging paper like a goddamned mummy and taped me up from my neck down to my ankles?"

"That's how we found him when we arrived here," Officer Gorshin said softly to Timmy.

"Who found you and called the police?" Timmy asked Stu.

"One of the guys that works here," Stu said, gesturing at a young black man standing nearby dressed all in white in baker's regalia. "That's Reggie, he's deaf. He had been heading outside to have a cigarette when he found me all trussed up on the floor. He got me loose and then I called the cops. So yes Soldier boy, I told the officer's here what happened."

Timmy glanced over at Reggie and the handsome black man held up a hand in polite greeting.

"Your feet are bare Stu, why is that?" Timmy asked, already knowing the answer.

"The guy who was the ringleader took my shoes and socks," Stu said angrily. "Can you beat that? What a shitty thing to do to a guy huh? I mean, they had robbed the vault, skimmed it clean, but then they had to take my damn shoes and socks too?"

Timmy knew that for some reason the young security guard was leaving out the fact that he had been tickle tortured.

"Uh Stu, can we start at the beginning for the officers here, and for me as well?" Timmy asked politely, pulling up a chair next to the security guard. "You see, I've sort of become involved in all this for reasons that I can't get into at the moment."

Stu looked at Timmy and saw in the soldier's eyes something akin to caring. For some reason the security guard knew he could trust this man...

"Yeah, sure," Stu said and Officer Romero quickly had his notebook and pen in hand.

"Start with your name again Stu," Timmy prodded gently.

At that moment two more bakers, one woman and one man made the scene, they heading outside for a break. When they saw the commotion going on they stopped in their tracks.

"It's okay folks, everything is under control here," Officer Gorshin stated with total authority.

The female baker looked at the blown vault, the distraught security guard and Reggie and said "Yeah right," but when she took in the sight of Timmy her eyes lit up…

As soon as the two bakers went outside on their break Timmy turned his attention back to Stu…

"My name is Stu Parker," the security guard said, sounding more respectful now as he looked in Timmy's eyes. "I work here part time as a security guard. I attend Claymore College."

"Okay Stu, go on," Timmy said.

"I was on duty here, about two hours ago three guys came waltzing in here, the ringleader, he was dressed up like a baker with dorky looking glasses on," Stu went on, describing Adam the tickle Meister. "I could tell he was disguised, didn't want anyone knowing who he really was… When I stood in their way he told me they were deliverymen. I knew that was a load of horseshit because we don't get deliveries on Saturday. Anyway, one of his two cohorts was filming him talking to me. Fuckers got me on tape…"

"Okay, so this time he disguised himself as a baker, probably figured it would gain him quicker access," Timmy said to Officer Gorshin as Officer Romero wrote in his notebook.

"And then they pied me man, right in the face they pied me twice," Stu said miserably. "Fucker said that the pies cured insomnia and by fuck he was right."

"What do you mean?" Timmy asked, looking at the remnants of cream still on Stu's face.

"I inhaled and swallowed some of the cream they pelted me with and the next thing I knew I was on the floor in a stupor," Stu replied. "I study chemistry. I know what chloroform smells like Soldier."

"Okay," Timmy said, knowing that now he was getting to the meat and potatoes of the story. "And what happened after that?"

"It was the sound of the vault being blown open that roused me from the stupor I had been pied into," the security guard said. "I was laying on my stomach on top of that table over there. The guy who called himself "The Meister", that's what the fuck he told me, jeez, he was using a wet cloth to wipe the cream off my face. Real considerate of him huh? When I went to jump the fucker was when I realized that I had been wrapped up in packaging paper and taped up too, real tight and secure let me tell you. Fuck man, I thought they were gonna kill me, maybe kidnap me. But who the fuck would kidnap a security guard?"

"Heh, who indeed?" Timmy asked softly, his mind once again on a man named Ronald Greene.

Timmy noted not only the remnants of pie cream on the security guard's face, but also the tatters of the duct tape that had been used to restrain him like a package.

"What uh, what all did they do to you while you were trussed up Stu?" Timmy asked.

"Well, before I get to that, I noticed that besides being all trussed up that my shoes and socks had been taken off my danged feet," Stu said. "The "Meister" had them on the table next to me. He thanked me for them and said they would be an addition to his collection. Now I ask you Soldier boy, what sort of guy keeps another guy's shoes and smelly socks?"

Timmy's cock churned...

"Well, I can tell you this much Stu," Timmy said. "The man we're dealing with is a serial type of suspect; he did this yesterday as well and kept the victim's shoes and socks. So you see he collects the shoes and socks as trophies of sorts..."

"Oh jeez, that's just too way out there for me," Stu said, nodding his head from side to side.

"So, can you tell me if you were violated in any manner while you were bonded?" Timmy asked the security guard, sounding as gentle as possible.

Stu looked up at the two cops and then back at Timmy, took a deep breath and said, "Yeah, but you won't believe it when I tell you."

"Try us," Officer Romero said with a grin.

Officer Gorshin turned to Romero and silenced him with a warning glare from his eyes.

"The guy, the ringleader, he told me to call him the Meister," Stu said. "When I asked him why I had to call him that he said this is the reason, and he held up a long sharp edged feather. It looked like a feather that might have fallen off a goose or even an eagle."

Timmy stifled a gulp and his head spun for a moment…

"Well, anyway, I found out real quickly why he wanted me to call him the Meister, seeing as he had me screaming that word and begging him to stop tickling my danged feet with that feather," Stu said. "Fuck, he tickled my feet and I could tell that my laughing like an out of control hyena had him boned up. And the guy with the cam filmed it all. He filmed them robbing the vault, he filmed me being tickled and he filmed me laughing and laughing. By the time they left me here the vault was emptied and I had tears of laughter running down my face…"

"Okay, thanks for your candor and openness Stu," Timmy said and turned to the officers.

"Have you two heard enough?"

"Yes, and like yesterday we'll have the kid checked out medically and we'll supply him with new shoes and socks," Officer Gorshin said.

Stu looked up at the three men and again rolled his eyes in disbelief…

While Timmy was taking the security guard's statement with Officers Gorshin and Romero the man named Adam, AKA the "Tickle Meister" was enjoying watching the latest video that he and his two cohorts had created earlier that day. The three men were seated in front of a television as the video of a packaged up security guard named Stu was feather tickled on his bare upturned feet and laughed crazily. The three men laughed along with their latest conquest, the Meister holding Stu's socks and shoes in his lap.

"Jeez Adam, this is all too much," James chuckled. "A fucking tickle epic, of all things, and dedicated to an author who writes about it…"

"Yes, yes," the Meister said, sounding fiendish, his cock churning in his pants as he continued watching the video. "And now that that soldier, Christopher Trevor's recurring character in numerous books has made the scene we should be able to finish this up sooner than I thought…"

"What do you mean?" Clyde asked.

"What I mean is, I did a little checking on the internet for military events in the immediate upcoming future," the Meister said, aimed a remote control at the television and muted it. "This Monday night there is going to be a reserve soldier's reunion gala at the "Embassy Hall", the famous catering establishment that has hosted those sorts of events for the last hundred years or so. I managed to hack into their guest list and Major Backman will be attending. And his guest list includes his wife and I'll give you both one guess between both of you who else is on the soldier's guest list."

Clyde and James looked at each other and said the name, "Christopher Trevor…" at the same time.

"Bingo, ding, ding, ding, you each win first and second prize," the Meister said, stood up and stepped over to a table where layers upon layers of cash was piled up. "But for tomorrow we have one more establishment to hit, seeing as we need more cash…"

Smiling fiendishly Adam the Tickle Meister held up a photo of a world famous library.

"But Adam, there won't be anyone at the library to film for another tickle scene," James said, stepping next to his tickle boss.

"Don't sound too disappointed James, because you see, what I plan to film at the library tomorrow will be the introduction of Christopher Trevor in my drama," the Meister said, squeezed the back of James' neck, aimed the remote control at the TV and resumed the tape of Stu laughing playing.

All three of the men laughed along with Stu on the tape…

Sunday morning found reserve soldier Timmy Backman on the phone with his author buddy Christopher Trevor. Timmy sat on his side of the bed wearing just his frosty white pouch style boxer briefs, quickly summarizing the police case he had become involved in.

"And whoever this guy is he calls himself the tickle Meister?" Christopher Trevor asked when Timmy had stopped speaking. "Hmm, no wonder it seems sort of ironic to you that you became involved in it."

"Yes, and my instinct tells me that these robberies and tickle assaults he's visited on unwitting victims is all a rouse of some sort for something much bigger," Timmy said.

"What do you suppose his true purpose is?" Christopher asked, pecking away at his computer keyboard as he spoke on the phone.

"I'm not sure yet, but I just figured that you would want to know about it, figuring it might be good story fodder for you," Timmy said, opening his sock drawer and pulling out a fresh pair of black socks for that day.

"I'm already taking notes," Christopher replied and as Timmy cradled the receiver against his ear and pulled his socks on he smiled as he heard Christopher's fingers pecking away at what seemed like bionic speed.

"Ha, ever the writer," Timmy said. "Just be sure to change all the names to protect the innocent huh bud?"

"Always," Christopher said. "Listen, I'll see you later for brunch, we're still getting together before the reunion tomorrow night, correct?"

"Sure thing bud," Timmy said. "You're going to love the celebration, lots of uniforms there, lots of inspiration for you."

"When it comes to uniforms you're the only inspiration I need Timmy," Christopher said softly.

The two men were silent for a few seconds, each of them not daring to say what was actually in their hearts and minds...

"Okay then, I'll see you later tonight for brunch," Timmy said.

"Sounds good," Christopher said and they hung up.

As Timmy stood up Stephanie was suddenly behind him...

He felt her thin arms entwine his upper torso. His cock was suddenly bulging in his boxer briefs.

"Well, well, good morning to you too my love," Timmy said breathlessly as Stephanie's fingers clasped his sensitive nipples...

Timmy leaned down and kissed Stephanie's wrists...

He then turned, enveloped her in his strong arms and they kissed passionately on the lips. Timmy knew that by the time he met his author buddy for brunch that day he would be very hungry indeed... Stephanie's hands found their way to the back of her husband's big neck and they kissed harder yet...

Later that afternoon Timmy and his author buddy Christopher Trevor were seated in a trendy restaurant enjoying a brunch of cheese omelets, French fries, champagne and orange juice beverages and coffee. Both men were casually dressed in jeans, pullover collared shirts and loafers.

"Amazing how this strange case of a serial thief and tickler cracked just as the reserve soldier gala is coming up," Christopher said, looking across adoringly at his good buddy.

"What do you mean buddy?" Timmy asked, putting down his coffee cup.

"Well, what better place for this guy to find new tickle victims?" Christopher asked. "And with me attending it would make for even more story telling, wouldn't you say?"

"Hmm, I hadn't thought of that," Timmy said and swallowed a mouthful of eggs. "You think maybe this guy and his video cohorts will try to crash the party tomorrow night?"

"Who knows?" Christopher said and bit into a French fry, chewed and swallowed. "I mean, think about it, me in town, this guy on the prowl, robbing famous establishments and tickling unwitting victims, filming it all, it all just seems too close for comfort. It really does sound like something I would be writing about…"

"Don't worry bud, this isn't one of your stories yet, I won't let anything happen to you," Timmy stated sternly.

"Well, I thank you for that my laddy," Christopher said with a grin and rubbed the tip of his shoed foot against Timmy's calf under the table.

"More coffee Sir?" the waitress asked Christopher as she suddenly appeared at the table.

"Yes, thank you, seeing as I'm driving I can't have any champagne so please keep the coffee coming," Christopher said.

"Not an issue," Timmy said. "You'll be able to drink all the champagne you want tomorrow night, I'll have a driver for you and everything…"

"Thanks so much Timmy," Christopher said and took a long gulp of the coffee. "And you know what else makes me think that this so called tickle Meister has me on his mind?"

"I know what you're going to say, that he keeps his tickle victim's shoes and socks after he's done with tormenting them," Timmy said.

Christopher looked across the table at his buddy and nodded.

"Kind of scary eh?" the author asked.

"More than kind of," Timmy replied. "I get the feeling that perhaps he's read your books and is using some of the stuff you've written about as guides to his crimes…"

"What a way to gain a fan," Christopher said dejectedly. "And I'm also thinking that perhaps I know who he really is."

"Who are you thinking about?" Timmy asked and the author simply nodded his head from side to side.

"I'm thinking I better be on my guard tomorrow night…or maybe not," Christopher mused. "Now, let's get done here because I want you to see the hotel room I got for the nights I'll be in town. It has a Jacuzzi in the bathroom, can you believe that my laddy?"

Timmy smiled knowingly at his author buddy and then his cell phone rang in his pocket. Timmy extracted the phone from his pocket, looked at the caller ID and said to Christopher, "Its Officer Gorshin…"

Christopher looked intently at his buddy as Timmy took the call.

"Yes Officer, I'll meet you there in about ten minutes," Timmy said and hung up after having a short chat with the cop. "I have to go. You finish up here, I'll try to come and see your hotel room later. If not I'll see you tomorrow at the reserve soldier's gala."

"Where are you off to?" Christopher asked as Timmy stood up and dropped a couple of bills on the table.

"The Midtown library, it's closed on Sunday's but it was robbed an hour ago," Timmy said. "Robbed of all the books written by Christopher Trevor..."

Christopher's jaw dropped as Timmy made his way out of the restaurant...

Ten minutes later Timmy and Officer Gorshin were in the section of the famous library marked, "Erotica and Adults only."

"How do we know he stole all the Christopher Trevor books?" Timmy asked the officer as they both squatted in front of an empty shelf among other shelves that were fully stocked.

"He left us a calling card this time," the cop said and handed Timmy a business card that was in a plastic sealed poly bag.

Timmy looked at the card in the evidence bag and nearly blanched when he saw the image of a masked man dressed all in black along with a top hat and holding a walking stick in one hand. In the man's other hand was a copy of Christopher Trevor's first book.

"This proves my theory," Timmy said despondently. "I'm really going to have to look out for Christopher Trevor tomorrow at the reserve soldier's reunion party. He's attending as one of my guests..."

As the two men were hunkered down at the bookshelf neither of them were aware of Clyde on the other side of the shelf, nor were they aware of the tiny camera that had been planted in the shelf of books behind them. They did not know that their conversation and everything they were doing was being videotaped and captured on film AND being transferred to the Tickle Meister's secret location... They also did not know that the Meister was at this moment watching them on his television. He watched with a look of anticipation etched on his face. Neither Officer Gorshin nor the cop saw Clyde as he started moving a stack of books off the shelf above them, a stack of books that when pushed would come tumbling down on the two unsuspecting men. The Tickle Meister was hard as steel in his pants as he listened to Timmy Backman talk about Christopher Trevor. Then, Clyde pushed the stack of books and quickly made his way out the back entrance of the library. The books came tumbling down in an avalanche manner, hitting the cop and Timmy square atop their heads.

"YOWWWW!" the two men roared in unison as they were book pummeled.

As Officer Gorshin's hat fell from his head and he landed on his back in one direction, Timmy landed in the opposite direction, both men's feet at the other's face. In his secret hideaway the Meister laughed uproariously. James chuckled behind his camera as the two men were knocked into a painful stupor…

James trotted over to the two men, filmed their sleeping faces and then made his departure behind Clyde from the library…

A few moments later Officer Gorshin awoke, murmuring, "Ohhhhhh jeez, what in the hell hit me?" As he sat up, rubbing his head as he did so he took in the fact that he was surrounded by books and also that his head was right next to Timmy's feet…

"SHIT, Major Backman," Officer Gorshin said, instantly concerned for the welfare of the man who had been assisting in this most profound of cases.

The cop's hat had taken much of the blow to his head whereas Timmy hadn't had any protective gear to soften the blow he had received.

Timmy moaned as he heard the officer saying his name and as the man lifted his upper body from the floor, gently patting him on the face.

"Major Backman, are you okay?" Officer Gorshin asked, checking to make sure there was no blood seeping from Timmy's scalp.

"Wh-what happened?" Timmy asked looking up in a daze as the cop cradled him. "What in tarnation hit us?"

"A stack of books Sir, it seems like our Meister knew we would be here," the cop stated. "Are you okay Major?"

"Y-yeah, no real damage done I don't think," Timmy said. "What about you?"

"I think I'll survive this little setback, only my pride was really wounded," the cop said and both men smiled and laughed a bit.

"Seems like this Meister is getting a bit too big for his bridges," Timmy said as he sat up in the cop's strong hold. "Funny, and no pun intended there, but he didn't tickle torture us, and we're both still wearing our shoes and socks…"

"Yeah, but somehow I get the feeling we were filmed," the cop said, looking around and then turning and looking directly into Timmy's eyes.

"I read one of the books you wrote with Christopher Trevor," the cop said softly and held Timmy tighter.

"Did you enjoy it?" Timmy asked in reply.

In response the cop clamped his mouth down on Timmy's...

"Oh my word..." Timmy said to himself...

While Timmy was kissed by Officer Gorshin the tickle Meister was looking at the copy of the invitation that Christopher Trevor had received for the gala the following evening. He smiled from ear to ear...

Sunday night found reserve soldier Timmy Backman, his wife Stephanie and his buddy Christopher Trevor all at the "Embassy" catering hall enjoying the festivities. Timmy had arrived ten minutes into the event with his wife and buddy, wanting not to make any kind of an entrance and wanting not to draw any attention to the author in attendance. Christopher really did not seem all that worried Timmy was glad to note. After all, this was the stuff that most of the author's tales were based, sinister happenings in an ordinary world. Timmy was dressed regally and handsomely in a fresh olive colored dress military uniform, Christopher was clad in a navy blue suit, very befitting a guest of the evening and Stephanie, Timmy's beautiful wife was sporting a red and white gown that really showed off her ample cleavage. Timmy considered himself a very lucky man this evening... The way some of his army buddies were checking out his wife and the way some of them were even checking out the author made Timmy feel on top of his game for sure...

"Everything seems to be in order," Christopher said, standing next to Timmy with a glass of champagne in hand.

"Yes, it does, for now," Timmy responded, looking around the huge room suspiciously.

Timmy's eyes fell upon Captain Robert Hayes, from the robbed movie theater just a few days prior. He at first didn't recognize the young man in his uniform. When Robert waved at Timmy and his wife and guest they politely waved back as Timmy informed Christopher who the handsome reserve soldier was...

While the festivities were slowly gearing up in the main room of the hall, in a private room down the hall the Meister had used his counterfeit invitation to gain entrance the back way. He had listed his two cohorts as his guests.

"Okay, now that we're here lets do what we came for and enjoy the results afterward," the man named Adam, known as the Tickle Meister said to his two cohorts.

He donned a pair of dark glasses and he, James and Clyde exited the private room...

As they walked down the hallway toward the main party room James detached himself from them and stepped into a luxurious bathroom… The Meister chuckled…

"So, are you enjoying yourself tonight Captain Hayes?" Timmy asked the young reserve soldier after having introduced him to Christopher and Stephanie.

"Yes Sir Major Backman, it's an honor to be here," the captain replied. "And I even get to meet a published author…"

Christopher smiled at the captain and thought about him being tied up and tickled at the movie theater a few days ago. He didn't seem all the worse for the wear it seemed to the author.

"So, I see you've recovered from your harrowing experience then," Christopher said to the captain.

"Yes, thank God I wasn't injured or worse, as Major Backman here so pointed out to me," Captain Hayes said.

"I see," Christopher said.

"Well, if you all will excuse me I think nature is calling a tad loudly at this point," Timmy said, holding up an empty champagne glass. "By any chance do you know where the nearest men's room is Captain Hayes?"

"Yes Sir Major Backman, right down that hallway on the left side," Captain Hayes replied. "Actually, if it's okay with you I think I'll join you. Champagne has a way of going right through me as well Sir…"

"If you will excuse me my dear," Timmy said to his wife and then gestured at Christopher.

As Timmy and Captain Hayes walked toward the men's room Stephanie said, "Come on Christopher, let's mingle a bit…"

"Sure, that sounds good," Christopher said and walked beside Stephanie to a refreshment table.

In the men's room Timmy and Captain Hayes were standing side by side at urinals, relieving themselves.

"AWWWW, that feels great," Timmy said huffily. "I almost didn't make it…"

Captain Hayes chuckled and said, "Yes sir, me too Major Backman…"

When Timmy was done he flushed the urinal, packed himself back into his uniform pants and glanced over at his still pissing urinal mate.

"I'll meet you back inside the hall," Timmy said.

"Yes Sir," the captain said and when Timmy turned around he found himself staring into the single eye of the cam that James was holding as he filmed the suddenly unwitting reserve soldier.

"Say, who are you and what's with the cam?" Timmy asked and James responded by giggling fiendishly. "Say, are you with the press or something? I don't recall seeing you in the itinerary for tonight…"

"Major Backman, Sir, please look over here," Captain Hayes said.

Without thinking Timmy looked over at the young soldier and his eyes opened wide in horror as a chloroform soaked cloth was suddenly pressed against his nose and mouth…

"RRRMMMFFFFF…" Timmy sputtered in shock…

Timmy struggled against Captain Hayes' iron-like grip as the guy held the cloth securely over his nose and mouth. Timmy danced and pirouetted a bit on his patent leather shoed feet and then his eyes slowly closed…

"RRRRRMMMFFF…" he garbled softly.

Captain Hayes hoisted Timmy to his tiptoes, held him tight and also held the chloroform soaked cloth to his nose and mouth.

James chuckled with glee behind his cam as Timmy sunk to the floor in a stupor…

James and Captain Hayes looked at each other and smiled…

While Timmy was being captured in the men's room Stephanie and Christopher were enjoying another glass of champagne each.

"Stephanie, don't you think that Captain Hayes seemed a bit too relaxed for someone who had been terrorized the way he was a few days ago?" Christopher asked his buddy's wife.

"Well, he's a trained reserve soldier, maybe he was able to get over it real quickly," Stephanie said.

"Yeah, maybe, or maybe not," Christopher mused and then saw Captain Hayes talking with a couple of his buddies. "I'll be right back Stephanie…"

Christopher made his way through the throng of people as the hall crowded up and then politely tapped Captain Hayes on the shoulder.

"Uh, Captain Hayes?" Christopher asked.

"Yes Mister Trevor?" Captain Hayes asked the author. "Can I help you with something?"

"Wasn't Major Backman with you?" Christopher asked.

The captain smiled and said, "Yes he was, but he uh, he got a little bit tied up…"

With that the captain turned back to the men he was talking to…

Christopher looked around the crowded room but did not see his buddy anywhere…

A chill crept up the author's spine…

A while later Timmy Backman slowly climbed out of the chloroform induced stupor he had been so savagely thrust into.

"Ohhhhhhh, ohhhhhh my word, what, what happened?" Timmy asked no one in particular as he woke up.

"Ah, so you are finally waking up my laddy?" Timmy heard a familiar voice asking him and felt the tip of a thin object being trailed over his chest.

Obviously he was laying down flat on his back. He was able to surmise that much so far. The last thing he recalled was going to use a men's room at the festive gala for reserve soldiers that he had been attending. Then, horror struck as Timmy recalled Captain Hayes using chloroform to force him in a stupor.

"Gentlemen, without any further ado I give you my favorite tickle character by Christopher Trevor and yours, army reserve soldier and high socked banking lawyer, Timothy Backman himself!" Timmy heard a high-pitched voice bellowing from somewhere above him. "And once more, the laddy will find as his head clears and as he comes to that he has stumbled *yet again* into tickle trouble, tickle torture or, more precisely, tickle hell!"

Looking up to where the voice was coming from Timmy saw through blurred vision a man clad all in black with a top hat and cape on as well. The man, whoever he was, was holding a walking stick of some kind. Timmy figured that that was what he had felt being trailed against his chest just scant moments ago… It was the same image he and Officer Gorshin had seen on the calling card that had been taken into evidence at the library. Thinking of the robbed library and being book clobbered and then kissed by the handsome Officer Gorshin Timmy felt his cock tingle a bit in his uniform trousers.

"T-tickle hell?" Timmy asked. "B-but the gala…wh-what happened?"

The man standing over Timmy hopped down to the floor and sidled up next to the prone reserve soldier.

"Your party invitation for the gala has been revoked Major Backman," the familiar voice said to Timmy, the tip of his walking stick now pressed against Timmy's nostrils. "I am the one who revoked it, ha, ha, ha for you my laddy…"

As Timmy's vision cleared he looked up and saw the man's face.

"Adam, Adam H! You monster! Holy crap and tarnation!" Timmy bellowed and when he attempted to sit up was when he realized that he was strapped down tight to a conveyer belt of some kind, his hands roped behind him as well. "What is this man?"

Grinning meanly down at his captured prey Adam raised his walking stick and used it as a pointer. He indicated James videotaping Timmy with his cam.

"Keep up the act my laddy, soon you'll be starring in a tickle tale all your own," Adam said and then trailed his walking stick tip over the knot in Timmy's tie.

"Act? What act? This is no act Adam!" Timmy bantered angrily. "Say, that guy with the cam was the one who was filming me in the men's room back at the gala..."

Timmy recalled the two tickle and robbery victims telling him how they had not only been tickle tortured but filmed as well...

"You've been asleep quite a while my boy, and please call me Tickle Meister," Adam chuckled as he trailed his walking stick tip down Timmy's chest area. "I do hope that I and my cohorts here have made you as comfortable as possible."

Timmy lifted his head and looked down and across at his strapped up body, his jaw dropped in horror...

"Comfortable? Adam, what in all hell is going on here? Let me up, NOW!" Timmy demanded. "And what's with this new title you've given yourself, a tickle Meister?"

In response Adam placed a hand behind Timmy's neck and helped the reserve soldier to lift his head a tad higher. The tickle Meister laughed an evil deep sounding laugh as he positioned Timmy's head so he could see what awaited him at the end of the conveyer belt he was trapped on.

"Adam, I am not comfortable, nor do I think this is funny," Timmy bantered. "You call being strapped up and restrained like this comfortable man? I am a United States reserve soldier, and I'm wearing a uniform to prove it, you can't have abducted me, oh my word!"

"Ah yes, you are fully awake now aren't you my laddy?" Adam asked his prey in a very thick accented upper class tone of voice, really putting on the act for Timmy it seemed.

The Tickle Meister trailed his walking stick dangerously close to Timmy's bulging crotch and forced him to look straight down to the end of the conveyer belt, his fingers twining in Timmy's soft hair...

"Ah, but Timmy my ticklish laddy, abducted you I have, and abducted you are in that you are now powerless to stop what I plan to do to you," the Meister laughed, leaning down, his lips close to Timmy's and then he turned and looked in the direction of the end of the conveyer belt. "I had planned this for Christopher Trevor, but you will do just as nicely my laddy! And as you can see, based on where your famous sexy feet are aimed my boy, you are about to be tickled beyond your wildest imagination."

"What all are you going on about?" Timmy asked his Southern accent quite thick now, given the peril he found himself in.

Timmy looked toward the end of the conveyer he was lying on and saw a large plastic box there. In the box was a sort of spindle device with what looked to be numerous sharp-edged feathers hanging off hooks at the ends of each spindle. Timmy realized quite quickly that a man's feet could easily fit within the confines of those spindles and the feathers spinning against that poor guy's feet would most definitely take the victim to tickle hell. The captured reserve soldier also noted that the pants legs of his uniform trousers had been folded and hiked up to just under his knees, really showing off his long black socks. Timmy's eyes opened wide in horror, James caught the laddy's look on film and Adam slowly lowered his captured reserve soldier's head back down. Timmy looked up at the ceiling and gulped hard... Timmy realized that army reserve soldier Captain Robert Hayes had been a plant, a plant to get him involved in this case, but the plot to abduct his author buddy Christopher Trevor had been twisted to him it seemed to Timmy now...

"I am about to not only test exactly how much resistance one of our boys in uniform can take my ticklish Timmy, but I am also going to capture one of the most famous ticklish men on film as he laughs his head off," the Meister said, pointing over at Clyde who was positioned at the control lever for the conveyer belt.

Clyde pushed the lever and at the same time Timmy started moving slowly toward the box that the spindled feathers were housed in and the feathers began rotating at a fast speed. Timmy felt his body lurch and the conveyer belt began its slow crawl toward that ominous box of spinning feathers. Timmy's head jerked up to see that it was in fact true; his socked feet were crawling right toward those danged spinning feathers. The reserve soldier gulped nervously.

"So tell me my laddy, are you a ticklish soldier boy?" the Meister asked, sounding totally fiendish now as he stood by Timmy's feet, and began unlacing the soldier's patent leather dress shoes.

"Hey! Whaaaat…Oh my word Adam, you know very good and well from Christopher Trevor just how very ticklish I am. DANG, knowing how ticklish I am, how can you do this? How can you do what you're about to do to me man?"

"How can I not?" the Meister responded and laughed his evil laugh, having now gotten both of Timmy's shoes unlaced. "How can I not tickle torture Christopher Trevor's greatest ticklish bud?"

"Adam, Christopher will get you back for this man! You won't get away with this! So, let's just stop this nonsense. Turn me loose and we can just go back to the gala and forget all this ever happened…okay?" Timmy bantered and watched as the Meister slid his army shoes off his feet, all the while he moved along on the conveyer belt, slowly toward eventual laughing doom.

"Ah, but as you can tell my soldier boy laddy, the real question of the moment is, will Christopher get you?" the Meister laughed, sniffed the insides of Timmy's shoes, dropped them on the floor and he and his two cohorts laughed evilly. "In just a few moments your feet will reach the rotating feathers…and there is no Christopher here to help you not sing your song of laughter for me…"

Timmy lifted his head again and watched as the Meister slowly began peeling his thin black socks from his big feet…

"NO, NO, ADAM, you bastard, don't do this to me man! You can't go through with this…oh, come on man!" Timmy grunted, laid his head back and off came his socks. "Adam, let me up, turn me loose man, oh my word, woe is me!"

"Ha, ha again for you my ticklish boy," the Meister laughed, holding up Timmy's wrinkled socks. "OTC's for the soldier boy tonight eh? Nice and formal I must say."

As the Meister sniffed Timmy's knee length black socks the reserve soldier struggled to no avail in the tight strapping bondage. His bared feet, sweaty and moist twitched and flopped around as he tried and tried to pry himself loose…

"OH MY WORD!" Timmy bantered yet again, his eyes horror-filled as he was transported closer and closer to the rotating feathers…

Timmy glanced over at Clyde as the guy stood by the control lever for the conveyer belt. The Meister again pointed at Clyde and as if he were a robot he pushed the control lever to the fastest setting. Timmy was thrust rapidly now toward the rotating feathers…

It started sort of slowly, but rapidly changed from a slight breeze on his now bare soles and toes…then the spinning feathers found their intended target and sucked Timmy's feet in it seemed. They began to frail Timmy's wrinkled soles with the fine, stiff fronds at their ends, some of those feathers getting and spinning beneath the bonded soldier boy's toes. Helpless to get out of the way some of the feathers splashed around the sides of Timmy's feet, some of them rotated and toyed with the tops of his feet. No part of the handsome reserve soldier's bare feet was left unattended. And then Timmy heard it… the sounds of a man in the throes of hideous laughter echoing loud and shrilly throughout the Tickle Meister's lair…

"HAR, HAR, HAR, HAR, HAR, HAR, HAR," was the sound Timmy found himself making then as his bare feet were sucked into the box of rotating feathers.

The conveyer belt seemed to have turned itself off, it somehow knowing that its passenger had arrived at his intended destination…

As Timmy lay there laughing, his feet dancing helplessly in the confines of the rotating feathers James filmed him, Clyde watched in awe and Adam the tickle Meister wondered how Christopher Trevor would feel if he could see his star now…

"Laugh Timmy, laugh," the Meister said, holding Timmy's shoes and socks in hand…

And poor Timmy followed orders well…for he laughed and laughed and laughed.

To be continued…

∎

The Meister
(Part Two)

While army reserve soldier "Timmy Backman" helplessly laughed and cawed as his feet were mercilessly tickle tortured his author buddy Christopher Trevor had summoned police officer Gorshin to the gala army reserve soldier reunion he had been invited to attend. After not being able to locate Timmy for the last half hour Christopher knew that his buddy had somehow been abducted by the serial thief and tickler that he had been trailing along with the handsome Officer Gorshin. How the tickle Meister had managed to snag Timmy was not a mystery to the author either. Not wanting to alarm Timmy's wife Stephanie just yet Christopher discreetly called the cop on his cell phone and told him to come to the gala in uniform so he would fit right in. Stephanie was enjoying herself with two very athletic looking female reserve soldiers who had seemed to have taken a shine to her. Christopher figured he would let Officer Gorshin tell Stephanie of Timmy's capture when the time was right. The author figured that if they could find out where the Meister had spirited Timmy off to there might not be any need to tell Stephanie of her handsome husband's abduction. But still, Christopher knew that that happening was a very remote possibility indeed. Christopher also knew that somewhere out there his good buddy was helplessly laughing his head off right now…

"I have to tell you man, I feel so bad," Officer Gorshin said as he and Christopher spoke privately in a corner, watching the goings on of the gala affair. "I'm the one who brought Major Backman into the fold on this case. When I had heard that Captain Hayes who works at the theater that was robbed was a reserve soldier and when I saw Timmy there I just figured…"

"It's not your fault Officer," Christopher said, cutting the uniformed man off in mid sentence. "But that guy over there, Captain Hayes, the one you just mentioned, I think it would be worth questioning him…"

"Why do you say that?" the cop asked.

"Somehow I think he helped whoever this tickle Meister is to capture Major Backman," Christopher replied. "He and Timmy went to use the men's room together earlier and that was the last anyone saw of Timmy…"

"Hmm, but Captain Hayes was a victim of the Meister as well Mister Trevor," the cop said. "Why would he aid in capturing a fellow officer, one that outranks him at that?"

"Why indeed?" Christopher asked. "Didn't you say that the Meister filmed all his tickle conquests?"

"He did at that," Officer Gorshin said.

"Then maybe, just maybe, in exchange for keeping the video footage of himself being tickled Captain Hayes agreed to help the Meister snag Timmy," Christopher said and the cop smiled. "What are you smiling about Officer Gorshin?"

"Well, you're a writer yes?" the cop asked.

"Yes, that is correct," Christopher replied as the cop tweaked the knot in the author's tie.

"Well, you sure as all hell do think like one," the cop said and he and Christopher chuckled in a good natured manner.

While Christopher and Officer Gorshin were conversing over Timmy's plight the reserve soldier himself was now a sweaty and laughing mess, as he lay still restrained on the conveyer belt, his bare feet trapped in the box of spinning feathers.

"HOOOO, HOO, HOO, HOOO, HOOO, HOOO, HOOO," Timmy was laughing now in a high pitched tone of voice.

On one side of the conveyer belt James stood with his cam pointed down at Timmy's face, capturing the laughing soldier's cackles and cries as the feathers did their work. Every few moments James panned his cam over Timmy's sweat sopped uniform, over his restrained and strapped down muscular body as he twitched in the tight bondage, until his cam filmed Timmy's dancing and darting feet as they were methodically tickle tortured. On the other side of the conveyer belt Clyde was leaning down over Timmy as he loosened the reserve soldier's tie, making sure he was able to gulp good breaths as he went on laughing and screaming.

"You really are the tickle star," James cooed, sounding almost romantic as he panned his cam at Timmy's scrunched up laughing face.

"HAAAA, HAAAAA, HAAAAA, HAAAAA, HAAAAA, HA!" was Timmy's reply.

"Jeez, this guy laughs better than all the ones the Meister snagged so far," Clyde said as he unbuttoned the first two buttons of Timmy's dress shirt. "There ya go Soldier boy, after you've laughed a while more we'll get you some water...maybe..."

"HAHAHAHAHA." Timmy cackled. "You bastards!"

From across the room, seated at a table the tickle Meister watched with an erection of steel in his pants as his captive laughed and laughed. Like most people out there who knew Timmy Backman the Meister found the reserve soldier to be irresistible for so many reasons. But alas, he knew the ticklish stars heart belonged to Christopher Trevor when it came to this erotic arena and no amount of tickle torturing him would sway that part of him. In frustration the Meister rapped his walking stick against the table and picked up a cell phone. James and Clyde looked over at the Meister as he again rapped his walking stick against the table.

"Turn off the spindles in ten minutes," he said to James and Clyde. "My ticklish star has a phone call to make..."

The Meister's eyes and Timmy's laugh filled ones met across the room...

As Timmy laughed and serenaded the tickle Meister and his two cohorts Stephanie was now making her way over to Christopher Trevor and Officer Gorshin.

"Officer Gorshin, how interesting to see you here tonight, I didn't know the military had invited police officers," Stephanie said, looking somewhat lustfully at the cop.

"They uh, they didn't Mrs. Backman," the cop said, his eyes darting from Christopher to the beautiful woman standing in front of him. "I was summoned here on official business."

"I see," Stephanie said and licked her lips. "Are you a reserve soldier by any chance?"

"Uh, no maam, I'm not," the cop said with a smile. "I uh, was called here by Mister Trevor because we can't seem to locate your husband at the moment..."

At the sound of those words Stephanie looked back and forth between the cop and the author.

"He went to the bathroom," Stephanie said.

"He never got back from the men's room maam," Officer Gorshin said and then he, Christopher and Stephanie looked around the huge room.

They saw couples dancing, old friends enjoying being reunited, men and women in uniform having drinks and enjoying finger foods...

"So uh, what do you suppose happened to that husband of mine?" Stephanie asked and at that moment the cell phone in Christopher Trevor's pocket sounded.

"Excuse me a moment," Christopher said and put the phone to his ear. "Hello?"

"Chris, Christopher, oh God, Christopher," the author heard his buddy Timmy drawling in his Southern accent, sounding like he was pleading, which, actually he was.

Timmy now lay at the end of the conveyer belt, his bare feet still in the box of feathers but the spindles having been turned off. He lay there strapped down as the tickle Meister held the phone to his ear while James filmed the latest scene.

"Timmy, is that you my laddy, er, I mean, buddy?" Christopher asked his heart racing just at the sound of his star's voice.

Christopher saw Stephanie's and Officer Gorshin's eyes light up at the sound of Timmy's name being spoken.

"Oh yes, yes, it's me man, oh man, you have to get me some help here, it, it's Adam, I can't believe it," Timmy bantered and as the Meister chuckled he slowly brought the tip of his walking stick to Timmy's face.

"Adam? Adam H. is the tickle Meister?" Christopher asked, astounded.

"Yes, yes, he had his goons and that danged Captain Reynolds snag my uniformed and high socked ass," Timmy pleaded. "He's, he's really got me in a tickle fix here Christopher…"

"Where is here Timmy?" Christopher asked, looking at Officer Gorshin as he asked Timmy about his whereabouts.

"I'm not rightly sure man, I was brought here while I was still out cold," Timmy replied miserably.

The Meister then smiled, said, "That will be all my laddy," and sprayed a goodly amount of knockout gas into Timmy's nostrils from the tip of his walking stick…

"OHHHHHHHHHHH…" Timmy groaned at the sickly sweet scent and his head spun.

As the phone was taken from his ear Timmy slumped back down, into a sleepy stupor…

"Timmy? Timmy are you there?" Christopher asked and heard the sound of insane laugher.

"Your laddy is mine now," the Meister cackled.

"Adam," Christopher whispered. "Adam, you will pay for this…"

Then, the line went dead and Christopher looked angrily over at Captain Robert Hayes. The reserve soldier looked a tad nervous then as Christopher, Officer Gorshin and Stephanie made their way over to him…

"All I know is that guy had a video of me that I wanted no one to see," Captain Hayes was saying a while later, seated in a private room of the gala hall while Officer Gorshin questioned him.

The cop had allowed Christopher and Stephanie to be present at the questioning as well.

"I especially didn't want my commanding officer seeing the goddamned video," the captain went on. "You see that guy that damned CO of mine, every chance he gets he ties and tickles me…"

Christopher was taking notes in his mind but at the same time he wanted to know where his good buddy was being held as a tickle captive…

"Oh jeez, this case becomes crazier and crazier with each passing moment," Officer Gorshin said. "So you're saying that the tickle Meister, this Adam person, he was blackmailing you?"

"Not at first," Captain Hayes said. "But when he learned that I was a reserve soldier yes and he used that to get close to Major Backman…"

At that point the soldier looked up at Christopher Trevor…

"He wanted you, but when he saw the opportunity to nab your soldier boy buddy and tickle torture him, as so many others have done…well…" the captain said.

Christopher simply stared at the handsome and innocent looking young man and then Stephanie said, "Never mind all this, and just tell us where my husband has been taken…"

"If I tell you will I still go to jail?" Captain Hayes asked.

"Have you heard me say that you were under arrest?" the cop asked. "Have I read you any rights?"

Just then there were two soft taps heard on the door and Officer Newmar entered the room in full uniform. She and Stephanie looked at each other, smiled meekly and then returned to the business at hand.

"Where is Timmy being held and tickle tortured?" Christopher asked Captain Hayes.

A short while later Officer Gorshin and Newmar pulled up in front of a closed down fashion warehouse on the west side of the city. In the back seat of their patrol car sat Christopher Trevor but not Stephanie. Officer Newmar had convinced Timmy's wife to remain at the gala with two other officers that had then been appointed to guarding Captain Hayes. Until Timmy had been rescued Officer Gorshin did not want the captain escaping and he did not want Timmy's wife placed in any danger either…

"So this is where the Tickle Meister has Timmy?" Christopher Trevor asked.

"According to Captain Reynolds, yes," Officer Gorshin said as the three of them slowly emerged from the cruiser. "Now let's be careful here…"

As they made their way into the closed down establishment neither of the officers had drawn their weapons. Based on what they know of Adam he was basically harmless, just a tickle fanatic gone a bit over the edge… Also, Captain Hayes had told them that the Meister would not hurt Timmy, he would tickle him till he laughed like a loon but he would not hurt the handsome guy…

"Soldier Backman?" Officer Gorshin then called out as with a flashlight drawn each he and Officer Newmar slowly scanned the place.

Christopher found a large voltage light-switch and with a latex gloved hand Officer Newmar moved it to the "On" position. The whole of the warehouse was lit up instantly. The smell of chloroform was in the air…

Christopher's eyes opened wide and he said, pointing, "Look!"

The two police officers looked where Christopher was pointing and there they saw a stretched out uniformed man, his bare feet trapped in what looked like some sort of mad scientist gizmo. The uniformed man was strapped down tight…

The two officers and Christopher dashed over to where the restrained man laid, Christopher being the first to reach him. As they leaned over him they saw a note pinned to the uniform jacket the man was wearing. Then, the two cops and Christopher looked at each other in dismay.

"He tricked us, it's not Timmy," Christopher said, looking down at the prone positioned what appeared to be a man. "It's a mannequin in an army uniform…"

In anger Christopher yanked the brown wig off the mannequin.

"No wonder he held Timmy here and tickled him here, plenty of mannequins in a fashion warehouse to fool us with," the author said miserably and dropped the wig on the floor. "It is Timmy's uniform though… I would be willing to bet that Captain Hayes knew that the Meister would have moved Timmy before we reached here…"

"What does the note say?" Officer Newmar asked.

Officer Gorshin leaned down and read, "Did you really think I would make it that easy for you Mister Trevor?" The two officers looked at Christopher and the author pursed his lips together angrily.

"We need to question Captain Hayes some more," Christopher said.

"We haven't charged him with anything, we really can't force him to talk," Officer Gorshin stated sadly.

Reaching into the box of feathers where the mannequin's feet were Christopher plucked one of the feathers and held it up.

"You may not be able to force him to talk, but I can," the author said, waving the feather.

As Officer Newmar looked at the feather she recalled the tickling she had endured at the hands and fingers of the kidnapped reserve soldier's wife. She shuddered a bit, but it went unnoticed…

A short while later Christopher was back in the cruiser with the two cops as they pulled away from the warehouse. The mannequin made up to look like Timmy Backman had been placed in the trunk of the car, as evidence. Like Timmy however the mannequin's feet were bare… From a window directly adjacent to the warehouse the tickle Meister watched and smiled meanly as the car took off…

"Well my laddy, it looks like you're in for more tickle fun," the Meister said, holding tight to a pair of black OTC dress socks.

When the two officers and Christopher arrived back at the gala they had Captain Hayes brought out to the cruiser where he could see the mannequin clad in Timmy's uniform, minus shoes and socks and underpants they noticed as well. They asked that Stephanie be kept inside, as the sight of a mannequin clad in her husband's uniform might prove to be just too much for her. The detained Captain Hayes looked woefully at the mannequin in the car, his own hands locked behind him in handcuffs.

"Did you know that while we were rescuing a mannequin that the tickle Meister would make off with Major Backman again?" Officer Gorshin asked the captain, thinking at that moment of the taste of Timmy's lips on his when they were back at the library after having been toppled over the head and momentarily knocked out cold.

"I wasn't sure," Captain Hayes said. "I only know some of what the Meister had planned for the author Christopher Trevor..."

Christopher looked at the reserve soldier and held up the long feather...

"The officers can't tickle the truth out of you friend, but I sure as hell can," Christopher stated sternly. "Major Backman means more to me than you or anyone will ever imagine. I want to know what twisted plan the Meister had for me that he twisted to my good buddy."

"Please, there's no need to tickle torture me," the captain said. "It was all about making a tickle epic, capturing and filming the author Christopher Trevor while he laughed his head off while being tickled. Adam, the tickle Meister thought it would make a great and twisted tale. But then he twisted it even more when Major Backman made the scene at the movie theater where I work from time to time..."

"Where does the Tickle Meister have Timmy now?" Officer Gorshin asked.

"I'm not sure, I only know some words he said when he was hatching the original plan to capture the reserve soldier here at the reunion," the captain said. "And he said it in a language not quite English..."

"What was it he said?" Officer Newmar asked. "I'm pretty well versed in most foreign languages.

"A travers, he said, Timmy would be a travers after he had tickled his bare feet with the spindles, he said he would strip the soldier's uniform off him and take him a travers," Captain Hayes said, sounding guilt riddled. "I'm so sorry for all this and I'm sorry for what I allowed to happen to Major Backman..."

"A travers means across," Officer Newmar said.

"Across, or a cross, could it mean that he planned to hook Timmy up to a Saint Andrew's cross and tickle torture him that way?" Christopher surmised.

"Or maybe a cross, meaning he planned to use a cross to tickle torture the reserve soldier," Officer Newmar offered next.

"Across, there was another fashion warehouse *across* from where the one we found the mannequin in was," Officer Gorshin said. "And that warehouse was used to store a lot of the plastic booths where models outfits were stored to protect them from the elements..."

Like Timmy, Christopher suddenly thought of Ronald Greene...

In his mind he saw the many, many devices that Ronald had used to tickle torture poor Timmy over time; he himself felt a pang of guilt for the many, many ways that he had thought to tickle the poor guy, but the pang was gone as soon as it had come...

"I'm heading back there," Christopher said. "As soon as I tell Stephanie that Timmy is okay I'll be on my way..."

"We're coming with you," Officer Gorshin said.

"No, stay here, this is going to be between me and Adam the tickle Meister..." Christopher said sternly and stomped back into the reception hall.

Meanwhile, while Christopher and the officers forced the truth from Captain Hayes Timmy now found himself being prepped and prepared for more tickle torments...

The reserve soldier was stripped of his uniform and wearing nothing more than his OTC black nylon socks, his pouch style frosty white briefs and a white cloth blindfold tied over his eyes... His wrists were crossed behind his back and bound up tight in mounds of white knotted rope. As he stood balanced on his "spot" where the Tickle Meister had positioned him Timmy cried out in sudden stinging pain as a pair of tit clamps were snapped onto his jutted up man tits. While Timmy was being held tickle captive James and Clyde had made good sport of sucking and tweaking the ticklish guy's ample sized nubs, what Timmy sometimes referred to as his man tits... The two men had made a contest out of seeing which of them could get the nub that they were sucking on Timmy's chest the most erect. All the while the two men played their tit game with his nipples Timmy's cock raged hard and stiff in his pouch style briefs... He had silently cursed Adam, the danged tickle Meister as he called himself for having left him alone with the tit hungry James and Clyde…and now that his nebulous nipples were truly oversized the tickle Meister thought how they would make a good attraction in the upcoming video segment.

"OUCH!" Timmy railed as the tit clamps locked tight around his beefy nubs. "What in all hell?"

"Just some jewelry for your nipples my ticklish laddy," the tickle Meister said, salivating over the wonderfully muscular sight of Timmy tied up, blindfolded and in just his underpants and socks.

Timmy's cock was rock hard from a mixture of fear, anger and tickle torment in his pouch style briefs. The tit clamps, once the pain from the sting had subsided only added to the erotic and frustrating joy that the tied and blindfolded guy was feeling in his briefs.

"Keep up the facial expressions my ticklish buddy, its all being captured on film, just as we captured you," the tickle Meister said, squeezing Timmy's upper arm as he held him fast in his marked spot.

"You're doing it to me again aren't you Adam?" Timmy asked through clenched teeth. "Filming me? And this time I'm stripped to my damned socks and shorts, humiliating!"

"You know back at the feather device your author friend Christopher Trevor showed up to rescue you," the Meister teased Timmy meanly, squeezing and kneading his upper arm in an almost loving fashion. "But instead he rescued a mannequin that I and my buddies had dressed up in your uniform, that's why you're so scantily and sexily clad right now. Ha, ha for you my laddy, while Christopher and the cops rescued the mannequin we made off again…*with you…*"

"Adam, if you know what's good for you you'll let me go, and right now and pronto at that," Timmy bantered, leaning his head close to Adam. "Clothe me up properly and allow me to be on my way. Fuck, you stripped me and put my military attire on a danged mannequin? Humiliating man!"

As Timmy spoke the Meister tweaked one of his clamped nipples, sending chills and thrills through Timmy's very being. Timmy turned his blindfolded head from side to side and the Meister said, "Face forward my laddy, the cam is running and filming you, let's be sure we get your good side." As Timmy grimaced miserably, did as he was told, the Meister laughed meanly.

"I can just imagine how much moola I'll be making when this tickle epic is done Timmy," the Meister said.

"Adam, all of this tickling and tormenting of me has made you mushy in the head," Timmy seethed and at that moment the Meister whipped the blindfold off his tickle captive.

Timmy allowed his eyes to adjust back to the light and when he saw the man-sized device in front of him he gulped loud and heartily. James chuckled behind his cam and moved in for a good close-up of Timmy's terror stricken face.

"It's my own invention my laddy," the tickle Meister said, holding Timmy tight now by his arm. "As you can tell I'm a big fan of the book "Timmy's Ticklish Trials" and Ronald Greene's inventions in that book."

What Timmy was looking at was a Plexiglas booth with air holes in the top portion of it. The bottom of it was what was so riveting to the poor captured reserve soldier and made his fear hard cock twitch like crazy in his pouch style underpants. He curled his toes back under his OTC black socks as he took in the fact that the floor of the Plexiglas booth was made of smooth, round metal balls…and all of those balls had tiny rounded beads on them, at least hundreds on each one it seemed to the now tickle/terror stricken reserve soldier.

"Question for you my ticklish Timmy, how long do you think you can stay balanced on those rollers once you're in there and they're rotating against your ticklish feet?" the tickle Meister asked Timmy, his lips pressed against Timmy's ear as he spoke and he held his arm tight. "Staying balanced while laughing your head off is going to be no easy chore for you I'm sure…"

Timmy huffed loudly and in total frustration as the man who had captured him tormented him verbally and handled him in a subtle but erotic fashion… Timmy's erect cock twitched in his pouch style briefs…

"And seeing as I'm going to be leaving those silky socks of yours on you, you know that the ticklish sensations will be astronomical Timmy my laddy," the tickle Meister chuckled, holding tighter yet to Timmy's upper arm, his tongue tip grazing Timmy's ear as he spoke. "Any tickle fetishist knows that if his feet are tickled while he's wearing silk socks the sensations will increase tenfold…"

"You won't earn a nickel tickling my danged silk socked feet Adam, none of this makes sense," Timmy hemmed miserably as he looked at the man sized booth.

"Correct my laddy of lads, not sense, dollars, many, many dollars when I put my tickle epic on the market," the Meister said and pointed at James as he filmed the unfolding segment in front of him. "Now my handsome reserve soldier, its time for you to take your place in your starring position…"

With that the Tickle Meister let go of Timmy's arm, stepped in front of him and in one quick pull had Timmy's underpants pulled down and they pooled around his socked ankles. Timmy's hard and stalked up cock pointed at heaven and his juicy balls dangled low between his thighs. Droplets of pre cum oozed from Timmy's wide sexy slit and the veins in his manhood were pronounced and thick.

"Damn you Adam," Timmy bantered, his Southern accent now coming in loud and clear as James filmed his erect state. "Got me starring in a danged porn movie here now… Fucking guy you are, you let me keep my danged socks on but you de-under-pant me? Humiliating!"

"From the looks of this skyscraper between your sexy legs I would say you can't wait to be tickle tortured again my laddy," the Tickle Meister snickered and gave Timmy's hardness a squeeze, causing the captured reserve soldier to gasp loudly.

Droplets of pre cum and beads of piss emanated from Timmy's wide sexy slit. With no choice in the matter Timmy stepped out of his now discarded underpants and the tickle Meister moved his captive closer to the Plexiglas booth. Clyde opened the door of it, making like a doorman of sorts, teasing Timmy. Timmy gulped hard again as Clyde teasingly said, "Hope you enjoy yourself in there Soldier boy," and he was moved inside the booth. The Meister closed and locked the door behind Timmy. The ticklish guy's socked feet felt tingly on the bottoms as he felt the tiny beads on the balls he was now standing on pressing against them. He watched through the Plexiglas as James filmed him standing there in his high socked nakedness. His hard cock oozed more droplets of pre cum and Timmy's nipples were sizzling in the confines of the tit clamps. He struggled fruitlessly to get his hands untied.

"Now my laddy, its time for you to go to laugh city again," the Meister taunted Timmy as he held up a remote control device, Timmy's discarded underpants sticking out of the Meister's front pocket.

At the sight of the remote control device Timmy thought of Ronald and hunched his broad shoulders up in apprehension…

"No Adam, please, don't…" Timmy mumbled miserably.

"And off you go my laddy…" the Meister chuckled and pressed a button marked "Start" on his remote control.

Suddenly, from the other side of the room a voice called out, "Adam! Stop this now!"

In the Plexiglas prison Timmy suddenly found himself trying to balance himself on his socked feet as the metal beaded balls started rotating.

"OH, oh my word, woe is me!" Timmy bantered as he danced stupidly and began laughing as the beads worked evil magic on the bottoms of his socked feet. "HAHAHAHAHA!"

As Timmy stared forward he could have sworn that he saw his good buddy Christopher Trevor and that hunky and handsome cop Officer Gorshin outside the booth he was in.

"HAHAHAHAHA!" Timmy laughed helplessly as he thrashed around on his socked feet atop the rollers.

The beaded rollers worked ticklish havoc on the bottoms of Timmy's black socked feet, causing the poor guy to thrash and laugh like a loon in his Plexiglas prison.

At the sight of Christopher and the cop the tickle Meister clenched his teeth and spat, "Curses!" He pointed his remote control device at the Plexiglas booth and pressed another button on it.

"Adam, NO, I said stop this!" Christopher called out as he and Officer Gorshin approached.

In the booth the rollers started spinning faster and Timmy had all to do now to maintain his balance.

"HAHAHAHAHA, Ch-Christopher, Off, Off, Officer G-Gorshin!" Timmy heaved loudly in his tickle prison. "H-he's ticklin' me, DANG! HE'S ticklin' my danged feet in here!"

At the sight of Timmy in his black socked nakedness Officer Gorshin's heart raced and broke, and there was no denying the searing he was feeling in his cock. The way Timmy's erect cock was bouncing and flouncing around with his ticklish gyrations was sexy, even though the poor guy was suffering the torments of what had to be unbelievable tickle tortures in that booth. The cop knew just how very ticklish the bottoms of his own feet were.

"Hold it right there Mister Meister!" Officer Gorshin called out to the tickle Meister and realized quickly how ridiculous that sounded.

While Christopher Trevor made his way over to the booth that Timmy was locked in James and Clyde made their way to an exit door, James taking his cam with him. The tickle Meister stood his ground as the cop stared him down. Officer Gorshin did not draw his weapon for it seemed that the man known as the Meister was not armed, except for a remote control device of some sort that he had in his hand.

"I'm placing you under arrest Sir," the cop said and Adam simply grinned.

"HAHAHAHAHA! OH MY WORD, get me out of here!" Timmy screeched, averting the cop's attention momentarily.

Officer Gorshin stole a glance at Timmy in the booth and Christopher outside the booth, the author trying very diligently and most unsuccessfully to pry the door open on the device. When he turned back to face the tickle Meister again, prepared to lock him in handcuffs he felt a deep dismay. The tickle Meister was gone along with his two goons...

"G-get me out of here! HAHAHAHAHA!" Timmy railed, pressing his muscular body up against one of the walls of his Plexiglas prison, his socked feet pressed hard against the tickly rollers. "PLEASE GUYS! I'm bein' tickled to death in here!"

Sweat poured off the trapped reserve soldier as he was again moved uncontrollably by the rollers and made to dance a tickle dance on his thin socked feet... His cock twitched and swung sexily and the chain on the tit clamps swung a bit as well, causing the tit clamps to really pull and chew on the poor laddie's nipples...

"Adam has the remote control device for this infernal gadget! He can turn it off! HAHAHAHAHA!" Timmy screamed as he was moved around in circles now. "OH MY WORD, these rollers have a mind of their own it seems..."

"Adam took the remote control device with him," Officer Gorshin said miserably as he joined Christopher in front of the booth.

"Well, I can't get this door open and without that remote control it looks like we won't be able to get Timmy out of there!" Christopher seethed and the sounds of Timmy's laughter grew louder.

The cop and Christopher watched as Timmy was spun on the rollers, he tried to maintain his balance and he was tickled relentlessly. It looked as if the beaded rollers were actually licking Timmy's socked feet...

"OH MY WORD, what am I going to do? HAHAHAHAHAHAHAHA!" Timmy crowed loudly as he spun in a clockwise direction and then a counter clockwise direction. "Please guys, get me out of here! HAHAHAHAHA!"

"I'll shoot the lock off the door," Officer Gorshin said, reaching for his holstered weapon.

"No, the way Timmy is being jostled around in there you're liable to hit him by accident!" Christopher said a look of terror in his eyes.

"Then how else are we going to get the guy out of there?" Officer Gorshin railed. "If he keeps laughing like that he may not be able to breathe at some point..."

"Maybe I can still catch Adam," Christopher said through clenched teeth and ran off in the direction of where he had seen Adam running.

"WH-where is he goin' Officer Gorshin?" Timmy keened, his muscular back pressed up against one of the walls in the Plexiglas booth.

Timmy's socked feet danced and kicked out in front of him as he was tickled, tickled, tickled...

"He's going to try to catch Adam and get the remote control device from him to turn off those rollers under your feet!" Officer Gorshin yelled, pounding helplessly on the door to the man sized booth.

"AAAAYYYRRRRRR, HAR, HAR, HAR, HAR, HAR, oh my word, by the time he catches that danged tickle Meister I'll have laughed myself into oblivion..." Timmy cried out.

"I have another idea Major Backman, hold on Sir, hold on," Officer Gorshin railed and yanked his gun from the holster.

"Wh-what all are you going to do?" Timmy called out in between laughing his head off. "HAHAHAHAHA! Y-you can't shoot at the lock...HAR, ha, ha, ha, ha!"

"I'm not going to shoot at all Major Backman," the cop grunted as he gripped his gun by the barrel. "I'm going to try to pound the lock off the door of this thing you're in!"

With that the cop started banging the butt of his gun earnestly against the lock of the Plexiglas booth. Slowly, the lock began to give...

Timmy watched through laugh tear filled eyes as the heroic cop was doing his best to free him. The tickled reserve soldier's socked feet were suddenly pressed hard against the rollers and he found himself sputtering and laughing like a loon... More dollops of pre cum oozed from Timmy's wide sexy slit... his man sized nipple tits seemed to bubble up as the tit clamps feasted on them...

"OH MY WORD, I'm in a state in here Officer Gorshin!" Timmy bantered and when the cop looked up he saw Timmy's piss slit staring at him.

The police officer salivated at the sight of Timmy is all his sweaty musculature as he stood there tied, heaving, his tits clamped and wearing just a pair of OTC black socks… Timmy's erect cock looked like a thing alive as it stared the cop in the face… The officer continued banging his gun against the lock of the booth, slowly but surely the lock was breaking and would fall off…

The cop held his gun tighter from the barrel side and pounded harder and harder at the lock on the booth, trying to jar it open that way. He knew that this was going to be harder to do than he had originally figured.

"Almost there Major Backman, I'm getting you, I'm getting you!" Officer Gorshin ranted, him also sweating now.

From inside the booth the sounds of a man helplessly laughing and cawing his head off grew louder…

Officer Gorshin pounded madly now on the lock on the Plexiglas door, determined to free Timmy…

"HAR, HAR, HAR, HAR, HAR, HAR, I-I feel my legs tingling from my toes all the way up to my thighs!" Timmy reeled through clenched teeth as he spun on the rollers. "Dang, these things are spinnin' me here Officer Gorshin, please hurry Sir!"

"I'm doing my best here Timmy!" the cop growled and pounded the butt of his gun harder against the lock.

"OOOOOOOOO, ohhhhhhhh…" Timmy groaned. "The feeling is unbelievable…every danged part of me is feeling alive and ticklish now!"

"OH GOD, here we go Timmy, a few more good poundings should do it and you'll be out of there!" the cop bellowed miserably, his arms aching at that point.

Down in the garage of the warehouse Christopher Trevor saw the tickle Meister and his two cohorts climbing into a big van-like truck. As the truck pulled away Christopher came into the garage…

He saw Adam in the driver's seat and called out his name in a rage, his own voice a snarl at this point.

"Adam, give me the remote control so we can free Timmy, now!" Christopher called out.

The tickle Meister pointed at the author called out, "We will meet again Mr. Trevor!" and pressed his foot against the gas pedal…

But just as the truck was about to roll out the entrance of the parking garage Officer's Newmar and Romero blocked it as they came upon the scene in their police cruiser. At the sight of the cruiser blocking his way the tickle Meister slammed his foot against the break pedal…

"Oh sweet balls, THANK GOD," Timmy called out as the lock fell off the door of his Plexiglas prison.

The handsome Officer Gorshin quickly re-holstered his weapon, yanked the door of the booth open and reached in with two hands. He grabbed the sweaty and tickled reserve soldier by his upper arms and with a show of awesome strength lifted him off the rollers that were so tormenting him...

"OH thank you Officer Gorshin, thank you Sir, ha, ha, ha, ha, ha, ha!" Timmy called out as the cop set him down gently on his socked feet.

"Easy Major Backman, easy Sir," the cop said and stepped behind Timmy to untie his hands. "You're still laughing a bit there Sir, the ticklers have stopped tormenting you..."

"Yes, yes, they've stopped, oh my word..." Timmy panted.

As he untied the reserve soldier's hands the cop could not take his eyes off Timmy's delectable ass globes...

When Timmy's hands were freed he massaged his wrists a bit and then with his fingers trembling he took the tit clamps off his nipples...

"OUCH!" Timmy cried.

"You'll be okay Sir, that's just the blood rushing back into your nubs," the officer said reassuringly and the two men looked at each other lustfully.

The cop looked around quickly to be sure he and Timmy were still alone for the moment. Then, he pulled the tickle weakened reserve soldier close to him and with no hesitation whatsoever clamped his mouth down fiercely on Timmy's. He kissed Timmy long and hard, his tongue probing the reserve soldier's mouth, tasting his gums. He gave Timmy's steely erection a few squeezes and twists, but not enough to get the guy off. The cop didn't want to make a mess after all...hardy har and har...

"Oh my word," Timmy whispered after the cop stopped kissing him and released his hold on him. "Thanks uh, thanks for getting me out of that danged predicament Officer..."

"Let me see about getting you a blanket Sir, I'm sure there's one in storage around here somewhere..."

A few moments later, as the cop was wrapping Timmy in a large white sheet Christopher Trevor came back into the warehouse with the remote control device in hand...

Oh man, thank God you're out of there Timmy," Christopher said as he approached Timmy and the cop.

"Where's the tickle Meister?" Officer Gorshin asked after fastening the ends of the sheet about Timmy's broad shoulders.

"Not to worry Officer Gorshin, your teammates Officer Newmar and Officer Romero have Adam, AKA the tickle Meister well in hand," Christopher said happily, stepping next to his favorite all time ticklish character. "Your uniform is out there in their cruiser as well Timmy... We need Officer Gorshin though to release it from evidence hold."

Timmy, standing there wrapped in a blanket and Christopher both looked at the cop.

"Think you could get me properly clothed Officer Gorshin?" Timmy asked the cop.

"I'll go and get your uniform Timmy," Officer Gorshin said, dashing out of the warehouse, leaving Timmy with his author buddy.

"I sort of get the feeling he likes you my laddy," Christopher said and smiled sexily at the sheet-wrapped Timmy, only his head and black socked feet showing.

"Do I detect a tad of jealousy in your voice bud?" Timmy asked Christopher.

Christopher smiled evilly and in a playful move loosened the sheet about Timmy's shoulders and let it fall to the floor.

"OH my word," Timmy bantered as the author grabbed his erect cock in hand and slurped on one of his nipples at the same time...

Timmy swooned as Christopher Sucked heartily at his nipple, stroking his cock at the same time.

"Oh my word," Timmy panted again. "What if Officer Gorshin sees this?"

"I'm sure he'll join in the fun my laddy, as I said, I get the feeling he likes you..." Christopher said and slurped at Timmy's other nipple then.

"Oh yes, but somehow I get the feeling you like me a tad more Mr. Author Sir," Timmy gasped as his cock stiffened more-so in his buddies' hand.

"Don't ever doubt it Timmy, don't ever doubt it," Christopher said and then a few scant minutes later Timmy was shooting his pent-up load as his author buddy scoffed it down his throat, sucking Timmy's cock at the same time, caressing his socked calves as he swallowed him in gulps.

Timmy was awash with goose bumps and sweating as he emptied his ball juice into Christopher's craw...

When Officer Gorshin walked back in with Timmy's uniform on a hanger Christopher was just smacking his lips and gulping down the last remnants of Timmy's jazz. At the sight of the officer Timmy quickly re-wrapped himself in the sheet, blushing as he did so…

A few hours later Timmy was back in uniform at the reserve soldier's reunion gala, his wife Stephanie on his arm.

"So what happened to Adam the tickle Meister?" Stephanie asked Timmy as they stood sipping drinks along with Christopher Trevor and Officers Newmar, Gorshin and Romero.

"Well, he really wasn't a dangerous sort of guy, just a guy who wanted to make a tickle video to end all tickle videos," Timmy said with a grin. "He figured that by using Christopher or even me as the final tickle victim in his so called epic he would be an overnight millionaire. I have to say the guy did have some really ingenious tickle devices. So with all that in mind we confiscated the videos he made and destroyed them. There's no danger of Captain Hayes being seen as a tickle victim or Stu the security guard from the bakery…or yours truly here…"

"And amen to that," Officer Gorshin said and raised his glass to Timmy.

Adam has to do a few months of community service and then he plans to start making a tickle video again, but the legal way, by hiring real models and actors, not kidnapping or shanghaiing them," Timmy went on. "And my word, as I said, he sure as hell does have some ingenious tickle devices. Sad to say I experienced some of them firsthand…and feet…"

At that Timmy and his gathering of friends and new acquaintances all laughed…

"Well, I'm just glad you're back safe and sound Major Backman," Officer Gorshin said and took Timmy by his arm as Stephanie let go of her handsome husband to again go and mingle a bit. "Come, I'll freshen up your drink for you Sir…"

"Well thank you kindly Officer," Timmy said with a grin as the cop led him to the open bar. "Somehow I get the feeling that we have the beginnings of a wonderful friendship here."

"I could not have stated it any better myself Major Backman Sir," Officer Gorshin said with a grin and held tighter to Timmy's arm.

■

About the Author

Christopher Trevor

Christopher Trevor was born in July 1963 and grew up in New York City. As soon as he was old enough to know how he began writing fiction and has been writing gay erotic/ fetish stories for the past ten to twelve years at this point. He became an avid reader as well from the time he knew how and reads everything from fiction, to non-fiction to biographies of interesting and unusual people, people who have made a difference or who have paved the way for others. Christopher attributes his writing artistic inspiration to artists such as Etienne, Tom of Finland, Tagame, The Hun, and most notably  Joe T, who Christopher has had the pleasure of speaking with and even meeting over the last few years. Christopher states, "Joe T encouraged me to write about my fetish because I was embarrassed about it at the time. Joe T said that when we are embarrassed about something that makes it even more enticing somehow." Christopher totally agreed and never stopped writing in this genre. Erotic writers who inspired Christopher Trevor were: Tom Shaw (author of "That Day at the Quarry"), C.S. White (author of Big Sur), Larry Townsend (author of countless erotic novels), and Mason Powell (author of the classic story "The Brig.")

Christopher discovered that not only did he enjoy writing erotic tales but that after his first bondage experience he had a genuine flair for it. Writing to erotic oriented magazines about his first bondage experience truly opened the floodgates for Christopher where this style of writing is concerned. Christopher thanks the handsome and muscular "Greg" for that experience way back in time. Christopher took "Creative Writing" courses every semester during his high school years and while other friends of his stopped writing what they loved to write about as time went on Christopher never let a day go by when he didn't write something... "I feel that if I don't write every day I will die," Christopher has said many times over.

Foot fetish stories and all things related; spanking fetish, erotic shaving, muscle bondage, tickle torture, and hardcore stories are just a few of the areas of gay eroticism that Christopher enjoys writing about and inspiring in others as well. As one internet buddy said to Christopher where the black socks fetish is concerned, "Until I started talking with you I never gave a thought to my socks when I got dressed for work in the morning. Now when I pull my dress socks on every morning I get a chill up my spine."

Christopher is proud of the erotic effect he has on people...

Christopher Trevor is also the author of:

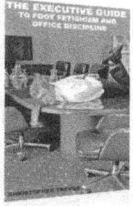 *The Executive Guide to Foot Fetishism and Office Discipline*

 *Timmy and The Hong Kong Tailor*

 *Executive Ties That Bind*

 *Love, Torture and Redemption*

 *Don't! Stop! That Tickles!*

 *Timmys Ticklish Trials*

 *The Taming of Dominick*

 *The Gym Instructor*

 *Milked*

 *The Military File*

 *Erotic Street Blues*

 *Quirks*

 *The Abusive Wager*

 *Timmy and the Evil Dr. Vonvellicator*

 *Terry's Appointment and Other Tickling Stories*

 *Blackmail*

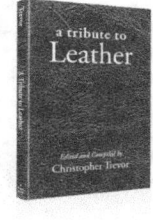